I0619268

Before We Thrived

Ballentine Lake Murray Southern Resilience Series, Volume 1

Deanna T. Cove

Published by Fountain Pen Harvest LLC, 2025.

BEFORE WE THRIVED

First edition. September 15, 2025.

Copyright © 2025 Deanna T. Cove.

ISBN: 979-8999942425

Written by Deanna T. Cove.

Table of Contents

Thank You God who leads me by his Spirit!

Thank you for your Mercy!

Dedicated to my husband who gave me a new laptop and told me to write. Thank you for your unwavering support, belief and devotion throughout our many years together.

...to my three adult children who are graciously navigating life.

...to my grandchildren...the small E's in my life and my sunshine!

...to both my parents and three siblings...my family for their love and support.

...to my coffee gathering friends and beta readers for your excitement, energy, devotion and encouragement!

...and to You!... my devoted reading fans and new readers who decided to give it a chance!

...She felt she had finally found her life's blessing and was also determined not to let any of her past interfere with the connection she had with Liam.

She thought what would be the point of flourishing after a painful childhood and leaving an emotionally abusive relationship, if your mind was still in bondage to them both.

She trusted his actions were for her best. Trust was the only thing she had energy for.

She would have life to the full promised to her; even after blood, tears and death; she would thrive...

Chapter One – The Life Altering Call

A lexie Branham, often called Lexie for short, noted the fine yellow dust of the season on her hands as she got into the car. It coated the walkway and all the neighbors' cars, as if sprinkled like a heavy seasoning from above. There was no point in washing her car just yet, she thought, staring out into the hazy spring air. Careful not to smear the pollen across her face, she wiped her hands vigorously on her leggings.

It was time to visit the closest home improvement store and the nursery on Highway Six, her favorites, with plenty of plantings and varieties awaiting her. She longed for the familiar smell again, the peace, and all the things that came with gardening that she wished she had discovered earlier in life. Maybe she had learned it at the perfect time; some things can only be appreciated in a particular season of life. She knew it was time to prepare for planting season, and she longed for it.

Since 2020, Lexie had taken on quite a few new hobbies to keep herself occupied during the period when schools were closed. She worked as a physical therapist within the school district, floating to fill staff needs. Now that life was almost normal again, aside from the high prices, she was eager to return to the parts of life she had once enjoyed. She had let her gardening go just a bit, but this was the season to start fresh, rekindle her love of growing things, and make time to walk outdoors again.

Treadmill season was over. Glancing into the overhead mirror, she decided she didn't care whether it was a good hair day. While waiting at the red light by the train tracks, she quickly French-braided her long dark-brown hair, snapped a rubber band at the end, and pulled out a few strands of her front bangs. It was a baseball-cap moment, and she was perfectly fine with that.

Irmo was a small but steadily growing suburban town, not far from where Alexie had grown up in Prosperity, South Carolina, a place even smaller. It was small enough for Alexie to run into Kevin at least once a month. They had met years ago in college and dated for a while after graduation. She had finally mustered the courage to walk away from his subtle but escalating emotional abuse. He never hit her with his hands, but his words and actions struck with blows that stung deep, deep enough to slowly crush her spirit over time. She was grateful he was out of her life, aside from the occasional run-ins that came with living in the same town. Run-ins that, lately, seemed to be happening more often.

It had been eighteen months, and she had finally moved on, from Kevin to Liam. She could trust someone again. Liam, also a close friend from college and once a work confidant, had seen through Kevin's tactics long before Alexie had. He had spent years gently encouraging her to leave for the sake of her well-being and mental health. With him, she finally found someone who valued her as she was, without asking her to change. Liam had been her best friend, guiding her through one of the hardest chapters of her life, and eventually became her fiancé. Kevin was now only a reminder of turmoil, a chapter she never wanted to revisit. At last, she felt peace and progress taking root in her life.

Perfect timing to do a little grocery shopping. Driving toward her local Kroger was also a sure sign of spring. Lavender wisteria drooping from the edge of the road provided the perfect backdrop for the season. The side street was lined with a neatly planted row of pink crepe myrtle trees. Crepe myrtles were her favorite, specifically the Muskogee variety, with its light lavender blooms. A sure sign that spring and summer were ushering themselves into the community.

Surely there wouldn't be many folks out and about at this time of day. Her eyes scanned the deli display for her favorite cuts when she flinched at the voice she heard coming down the aisle toward the counter. Lexie lowered her head and quickly pushed her cart toward the dairy section.

"Lexie? I thought that was you. I almost walked right by. You okay? You look exhausted and worn down! Guess you've been working more now since we broke up. Hey, it didn't have to be this way. You know I was never gonna" Kevin said, dripping with false concern.

"Never would've what? I can't believe you would actually say it!... I'm fine. I'm at peace and finally feeling like myself. I gotta run," Lexie said.

She pushed her cart around him and headed for the front of the store, leaving her items behind as she walked out. Her heart beat fast, yet she felt as if she were moving in slow motion toward her car. Once inside, she stared up at the ceiling and breathed deeply until she slowly calmed.

She pulled down the visor mirror and studied her eyes, her slight crow's feet, wondering if she really looked that bad. She rummaged through the bottom of her purse for lip gloss and thought about letting her hair down, but then she remembered who she was dealing with. She shoved the gloss back into the side zipper and drove off. Maybe it wasn't perfect timing after all.

Nothing like Kevin to ruin the mood of the day. Lexie ended up driving for what felt like hours to another store just to avoid the chance of running into him again. When she finally got home, she sat in silence for hours replaying the encounter as the ice cream melted and ran over the kitchen island countertop. She was startled back to reality by the slam of a car door. Peeking through the blinds, she saw Liam walking up the walkway.

"Hey, are you okay? I called several times with no answer, so I thought I'd come by to make sure you were good." He glanced at the pile of groceries on the island and began putting away the items that hadn't spoiled. "You ran into him again. You know we really need to keep track of where he shops so you can avoid those spots, so you won't have to deal with him or his sarcasm. I've got two more years on this contract, and maybe after we're married we can find a place on the other side of town and finally be free from running into him. Did he get out of line? What did he say this time? What can I do?" Liam asked, searching for napkins to wipe up the melted ice cream.

"I'll be okay in a bit. Thanks for coming by," Lexie said.

That was Liam's cue to give her space until she processed the encounter. Kevin and Alexie had dated long before Liam, long before her new life as a Christian. Alexie referred to that relationship as her BC days: Before Christ, before she committed her life to her faith and truly began trusting God's direction. She was grateful to leave behind her old life of insecurities, iniquities, and emotional abuse. It wasn't perfect, but it was growth. She didn't miss a single second spent with Kevin, though he still believed he could win her back.

Liam and Alexie had known each other for years but grew closer after joining the new Christian Bible class at church. Both had walked away from their old lifestyles and started a relationship built on genuine friendship and shared values. Liam was everything Kevin wasn't. With him, she could be her raw, honest self. They were learning each other well, and their relationship would soon be tested in unexpected ways.

It was rare for him to just stop by. After he left, she checked the many missed messages from Liam and others. What she thought had been fifteen minutes was actually two and a half hours lost staring into space. She noticed a voicemail from her childhood neighbor; someone she hadn't spoken to in a while.

"Hey there, Ms. Shelby. I'm sorry I missed your call. Is everything okay?" Lexie asked.

"Well, I'm glad you called back. When was the last time you talked with your mama? I think you need to come by. I'm concerned about Christine. She isn't herself. I think she needs some help."

"Help? Help in what way? Is she sick? I intended to come up soon. I've just been busy with work. I'll come up this weekend," Lexie said.

"This weekend? Honey, you need to come today, or I'll have to call somebody else to check on her. She can't be alone like this. Now who you want me to call?" Ms. Shelby asked.

"Okay. I'm on my way," Lexie said.

Chapter Two-
Daughtering From a
Distance-Christine

L exie usually called Christine twice a month. Their conversations were so brief she hadn't noticed her mother's decline. Lexie's father had died when she was only six—from cardiac arrest on the way to pick her up from school. He crashed while driving. Her mother had never been the same since. Before her father died, she had been a bubbly, fun-loving mom.

Lexie had barely seen her smile since that day. She'd turned into a bitter, grieving woman who was never able to move on. She often deflected her grief onto Lexie throughout her childhood and especially during her teenage years. Lexie visited out of obligation, sticking to a schedule only when necessary as an only child. She checked on her mother in spurts—quick contacts meant to reassure herself she'd fulfilled her daughterly duties.

As Lexie drove up the driveway, she noticed the main door wide open with the screen door closed but unlocked. She stepped inside and scanned the pale blue walls with their tiny white flower print. Her eyes landed on a picture of herself and her father—her arms wrapped tightly around his neck as he carried her on his hip, her mother beside them wearing a big, bright smile.

He always smelled faintly of barbecue smoke. The photo brought back a warm yet fading memory of him. As she walked farther into the house, the putrid scent of spoiled trash hit her. She called out for her mother. Christine appeared in the hallway wearing three jackets and two hats pulled firmly down to her brow. She looked at Lexie with confusion.

"Who's that? I was waiting for Alexie. What do you want, and why are you in my house?" Christine asked.

"Mom? It's me. Lexie. It's only been a few months..."

Christine peered at her from halfway down the hallway. "Oh, Lexie! Come here and give your mother a hug! Hurry up...the baby's crying and I need to feed him." Her eyes brightened as she approached Lexie, hugging her neck and kissing her cheek with a big, warm smile.

Lexie stood still, her body stiffening under her mother's embrace.

"Mom, are you okay? What baby? I'm grown now. There is no baby." She gently removed the hats and a couple of the jackets. "It's warm outside. Why do you have on so many clothes?" Christine rambled on about snow coming soon while Lexie walked into the kitchen. Dirty dishes were piled along the countertops and in the sink. Trash was scattered across the floor around an overflowing bag, with a line of ants marching in from the back door.

After spending hours cleaning and throwing away spoiled food, she packed Christine an overnight bag and led her back to the car, Christine clinging to her elbow. Ms. Shelby slipped her hand through the crack of her front door and waved, watching them from her porch before closing the door behind her. The sun flickered in Lexie's eyes as she took the scenic route home—rolling green hills, occasional brown farm fences, herds of pigs and cows, and a few grazing goats along the way.

Her mother slept in the back seat. Lexie kept glancing into the rearview mirror, checking for signs of her waking. Christine slept deeply, as if she hadn't rested in days. Lexie saw traces of herself in her mother's wrinkled, worn face. Her hair was slightly matted and tangled. She held a tan-and-black plaid hat against her chest as she let out a gentle snore.

Alexie's mind was filled with anxious, worrisome thoughts. She turned on the car radio and breathed deeply through pursed lips as Christine continued to snore in the back seat. She didn't remember driving over the small, narrow bridge on the way home, where barely two cars could cross at the same time. She expected to see it, but the small goat pen on the right told her she had already passed over it—her mind numb from trying to process what was happening with her mother.

Lexie could hardly believe how pleasant her mother's personality seemed, considering how mean and gruff she had been throughout most of Lexie's childhood. Hugging her mother felt awkward; she hadn't experienced warmth from her since she was six years old. Where was the angry, sarcastic, critical mother of her youth? Lexie would have to adjust to this new, kind-hearted yet confused woman. *What a perfect time for her mother to fall into dementia,* she thought, *just as my life has begun to turn around.* She was engaged to a great guy, and now she had to explain that she was moving in with a mother in mental decline.

Lexie had mastered distant care for her mother: scheduled short calls, occasional visits, and a few mailed gifts. Spending prolonged time with her mother had always felt almost terrifying. Picking out a Mother's Day card took longer than it should.

Whenever she visited, her mother criticized her the moment she walked through the door, never asking how she was doing. Alexie had learned the art of tuning out those negative comments during her very short visits.

Alexie felt her mother was the most miserable person she had ever known. In her BC days, she had done whatever was necessary to avoid her mother's wrath. Now that she had discovered a new way of life, she wanted to figure out how to love unconditionally. Though cruel at times, she was still her mother. She had only changed after her father's passing. Alexie felt sympathy for her mother's deep grief, brought on by the sudden death of her husband. It was the only reason she had felt the need to maintain some kind of connection after leaving home for college.

She had a few happy memories, mostly from her younger years. Her mother's erratic behavior had resembled that of an alcoholic after her father's death—but she didn't drink. Lexie had self-diagnosed her mother with a mental breakdown many years ago. Christine refused to get help, keeping her emotions bottled up until she exploded weekly onto Lexie. That night, Lexie stared at the ceiling, anxious about Liam's response. She feared rejection, knowing her upcoming marriage now came with a mother in dementia to care for. Her mind barely let her sleep.

Chapter Three- Liam's Introduction

"Liam, this is my mom... Christine. Mom, this is my fiancé—you know, the one I told you about," said Lexie.

Christine made her way across the living room with her plaid hat perched over brown hair and her shirt slightly misbuttoned. Curiously, she touched the side of Liam's face and shuffled his dark wavy hair.

"Don't keep her out too late! She mentioned you were taking good care of her. I need to go get her a pretty prom dress for the prom!" Christine said, walking back to her chair near the window while shuffling her mail and mumbling to herself.

Lexie and Liam moved into the kitchen to talk. Lexie wondered what he was thinking—how he would perceive her mother's unexpected arrival into their lives.

"Your mom is a lot more pleasant than I expected. Did the doctors say how advanced her dementia is? I'm worried about you getting burned out. This kind of caretaking is really taxing," Liam said.

"They said she's declining rapidly, and yes... care will get harder. This isn't really my mom in the same sense—she has a new, pleasant personality. I don't know if I could handle it if she were the mom I grew up with. So, are you okay with all of this? Our lives would be completely different. She still has some cash in her account and a decent Social Security check. I could use it to find a sitter at least three days a week to get a break. We'd need adult day care or a long-term sitter if I went back to work. I had planned to return to the school after summer break. They're okay with me taking a short leave since I'm a floating therapist for the district. I need to figure something out. I need to take her to get her hair cut... it's a matted mess," Lexie said, her brown eyes filling with tears as her racing thoughts spilled over.

Liam reached across the table and squeezed her hand, playing with the ring he had given her. "We can do this. WE'll figure it out. I just need a little time to sort out the financials. Don't worry. What does she need? I'm about to run to Wally's in a bit. Anything to make her more comfortable? And honestly... this personality change is a good thing. It would've been really hard on you if she were the old Christine you told me about."

Alexie didn't respond. She wanted to tell him she had already investigated dementia facilities. In her mind, she still questioned if she could care for the mother who had neglected and abused her most of her life—even if doing so was the right thing. This new personality shift might be the silver lining of her mother's dementia. Maybe it was her mother's upbringing that caused her not to know better. She had given Kevin the same excuse for far too long.

One thing was certain: she couldn't choose her mother or her father's untimely death. But Kevin had been different. She had allowed an abusive Kevin into her life—but she had finally broken free. Now, she pondered whether she could care for her mother despite the scars—some visible, some not. Could she care for a mom who hadn't cared for her properly as a child? She decided she couldn't let it interfere with her newfound happiness with Liam, even amid the endless "what ifs."

As they left the kitchen, Liam stopped and stood in front of her. She met his eyes with a sigh of relief, braided her hair, and twisted it into a bun. "Time to get to work finding a sitter! Thank you. I wasn't sure how you'd react. I know you didn't sign up for all this. I need to start by cleaning out a closet for her."

"I signed up for whatever comes along with you. She's your mom. We'll figure it out. Let's just get her settled and comfortable for now."

Liam wasn't aware of all the details of her childhood—just the broad strokes she had shared. He didn't know every detail, but he observed enough to understand. He patiently waited for her timing to discuss anything involving her past.

He understood her need for patience and calm. Liam had battled his own troubled past, including a difficult marriage and his own BC days. Liam reminded Alexie slightly of her father in appearance—athletic, handsome, dark wavy hair, a short, well-groomed beard. He sometimes demanded unwanted attention when he entered a room.

He was devoted to God in a way that protected the purity of their relationship. They had vowed to wait until marriage, which became increasingly difficult as their love deepened. Liam felt the urge to leave quickly whenever they were alone at either house, which was rare. They spent a lot of time "alone in public," as they called it—long walks in parks, hours in coffee shops and restaurants until the staff began sweeping and wiping tables to close. Not much longer until their wedding day, they both thought.

Once done talking, Liam headed out to grab a few items from the store. Lexie watched him get into his car with a sigh of relief and a feeling she couldn't quite define. Lexie wasn't good at expressing her emotions—it always took her a minute. Sometimes she relied on her phone emojis, pointing to the one that matched her mood, much like she did with her students when using the facial expression pain scale chart. She wasn't sure there was an emoji for this feeling, but she knew it brought a calming sense of peace—and she felt it often with Liam. Something she had never experienced with Kevin or anyone else.

Chapter Four- The Old Christine

Lexie was in the kitchen making sandwiches for herself and her mother when she heard her mom yell sharply, "Alexie Branham! Get out here now!"

Lexie froze. She slowly rolled the fresh lemons across the granite countertop. She didn't remember making the lemonade and had to taste it to see if she had added sugar. Her hands trembled as she poured her mother's drink. Placing both hands on the counter, she lowered her head and flashed back to when she was fourteen.

Alexie lay in her bedroom, staring at the ceiling and holding her urine as long as she could. She glanced at the clock: 3:48 a.m. She couldn't wait any longer. Tiptoeing to the doorway, she saw her mother asleep, fully clothed, on top of the covers in the adjacent room.

Alexie's eyes scanned the hardwood floor. She knew which planks creaked the most. Carefully, she put one foot in front of the other, stopping on a dark brown plank that groaned beneath her weight.

Her mother rolled over near the heap of clean, unfolded laundry. Alexie quickly hopped to the bathroom, leaving the door open to avoid squeaks. First, she rolled off enough toilet paper to muffle the sound of her stream. She finished and tiptoed back to her bedroom. The routine was always to flush in the morning to avoid waking her mother.

Rushing past her dresser, she knocked her book to the floor with a loud *THUD!*

"ALEXIE BRANHAM! IS THAT YOU? What are you doing up? You scared me to death! You know I always think somebody's breaking in here! I told you to pee before bed and not wake me up! You could've flushed the toilet so I would know it was you!" Her mother's teeth were clenched, her lips pursed, as she picked up the hardback book and hurled it with all her strength at Alexie, hitting her in the face. Alexie covered her eye, tears welling.

"The last time I flushed in the middle of the night, you said it scared you to death! I was just trying not to wake you up!" she quavered, holding her throbbing eyebrow.

"JUST GO TO BED AND DON'T GET UP NO MORE FOR ANYTHING!" Her mother stormed back to her room, leaving the hall light on this time, seemingly oblivious—or indifferent—to Alexie's injury.

The scream of Alexie's name snapped her out of childhood memories and back to the present.

Alexie knew her mother's personality was back. Only the old Christine had that tone—the tone of anger and distress, of despair and fear, of sporadic, unpredictable abuse. Kinda like a louder, more forthright version of Kevin, but different.

Alexie gathered the food she had placed on a light blue, intricately carved eating tray. As she walked down the hallway toward the living room, she stopped to look into the hallway mirror. She studied the small, visible scar above her left eyebrow from eighteen years ago—the one usually filled in with eyeliner, preventing her eyebrow from connecting.

Alexie decided she would give her mother the meal and finally ask her to stop yelling and screaming. She was a grown woman now—thirty-two years old, to be exact. It was time to be treated as such. Time to do something about it and stand up for herself.

She entered the living room doorway.

"It took you long enough," said Christine, scowling with piercing eyes.

Alexie knew from her mother's expression that the old Christine was definitely back. Inside, she tried to resist trembling. Alexie turned away, placed the tray on the end table, and stirred her fresh lemonade before handing it to her. She kept her gaze toward the floor, silently praying she could speak in a way that commanded respect while remaining respectful.

"What a beautiful tray! I used to have one just like it. We must shop at the same place. You have the most gorgeous eyes. You look familiar. Thank you! So sweet of you to bring me a bite to eat. What's your name again, dear?" Christine said, offering an unfamiliar smile while gently rubbing the side of her hand as she took the glass of lemonade from Alexie.

Alexie pulled her hand back quickly after the transfer. The old Christine was gone just that fast. She considered giving her mother a few old photo albums to keep her occupied while she did chores, but instead, she gave her some women's magazines. She needed to start preparing the house for Liam to move in after the wedding and had much to do. Showing old photo albums could trigger Christine's old personality—best avoided.

Alexie found other ways to keep Christine pleasantly busy for the rest of the day: colored yarn of many textures, new magazines to flip through, and music from her era. Music put Christine in a head-bopping, dancing mood for hours without bringing back the old personality. Alexie wondered if music had always been a soother for her mother, back when she had been happier—before Alexie's time. At this point, it was about whatever worked to keep her mother busy, tolerable and pleasant.

Chapter Five – Friends and Plant Parties

Alexie looked out the back door window and admired the beautiful weather for a few minutes as a soft wind rustled the tree leaves. She texted Carla after tying her walking shoes.

"Hey Carla. Can we meet at the park across from the animal hospital? I finally got a reliable sitter for my mom. I need to walk away some stress!" she texted.

"Hey, yeah, Moore Park! I'm glad you can finally get away and out of the house. I'll see you at eleven. Renee asked if she could join us for lunch to start discussing wedding ideas. Is that time good?" Carla replied.

"Looking forward to hanging out with both of y'all! See you then," Alexie texted.

Alexie left early to visit the local nurseries, looking for plants to add to her garden and along her fence. She thought, *What's the point of having a privacy fence if our neighbors can still peek in while I garden?* She was looking for fast-growing flowering bushes to quickly add at least three to six feet of height along the fence.

It wasn't just about privacy; she also wanted a scenic garden atmosphere in her somewhat large backyard. The downside was that six neighbors could peek into her yard from their two-story windows. She was determined to fix the problem and create a natural backyard haven—something that would make her feel like she was in a real garden, like the ones at the local zoo. She planned to choose evergreens that wouldn't lose their leaves in the fall.

She parked and made her way to the nursery's side entrance. This newfound love of gardening made Alexie feel alive and gave her peace. Today, she planned to spend less than two hundred dollars on a few bushes and maybe squeeze in another Crepe Myrtle tree. They weren't evergreen, but their bright summer blooms were beautiful. She sprinkled them throughout the backyard, where she already had five, and searched for a spot for one more.

She entered the nursery and admired the chimes and yard furnishings. Huge, colorful pots lined the left side, while specialty soils for optimal crops sat near the register and entryways. She inhaled the earthy scent of raw dirt, her excitement growing. She would soon have a birthday, and all her friends would likely gift her certificates for the local nurseries and hardware stores, allowing her to indulge her planting passion.

She walked past a row of Sky Pencil Japanese Holly shrubs. She already had a row of these, though one had turned brown and died—on her replacement list for next month. Her row of Cleyera Japonica shrubs had rounded out nicely after a few trimmings.

Moving to the next row, she was immediately captivated by the intoxicating scent of the multi-sized tea olive bushes. She lingered for five minutes, thinking this must be what heaven smells like. She selected a shiny green-leaf bush with tiny white flowers, determined to make it the seasonal scent of her backyard and porch.

"Oh no, look at the time! Miss Tess, can I get two of these tea olives? And do y'all have any of those pink fringe flowering bushes with the deep purple and green leaves...are they called Jazz Hands?" Alexie asked.

"You mean the loropetalum plants? We have a few left in the very back row. The Jazz Hands version will be in about two weeks. Let me grab you a cart, sweetie! Where have you been? I haven't seen you in a while. I knew you'd be the first one here once the season started," Tess said, wiping dirt on her apron.

"I've had some family issues going on. I've been taking care of my mom. But you should've known I wouldn't stay away from the tea olives too long. I wish I could bottle it up and make perfumes and candles from it!" Alexie said.

"Somebody has probably already beaten you to it! But not a bad idea. I hope your mom gets better soon. Come in soon and see the blueberry bushes. You'll need to get two at a time!" Tess said, repositioning her hat and wiping sweat from her brow.

Alexie had once referred to Tess, as she was sometimes called, as "the little flower lady," until learning her name. Tess was short, with blonde hair and tanned from working outdoors, strong legs carrying her through the day. Most days, she squatted to tend the plants, always smiling with a great attitude. She had been a source of guidance and encouragement when Alexie first started gardening.

During the pandemic, Tess had become a friend and horticulture mentor to Alexie, as the nursery was one of the few safe outdoor spots to shop. Alexie occasionally imagined working at the nursery herself. The pay would be a fraction of what she earned as a school district physical therapist, but she loved the hours lost in dirt and calm. Maybe one day.

As Alexie eased into the parking lot of the park, she spotted Carla already on the walking trail, wearing a bright yellow tunic shirt and black leggings, her hat pulled down over her long dark brown hair. A water bottle rested in her hand, her small freckles visible, makeup-free today. Carla, Renee, and Alexie had been college dorm roommates and had remained close friends through the ups and downs of life.

Alexie jogged briskly to catch up.

"Hey! I was trying to get here. You know I always get hung up at the nursery—they've got all the seasonal things! I could spot you a mile away with your bright fanny pack and shirt! How've you been this week?" Alexie called.

They stopped and stretched on a bench before beginning their walk.

"Yeah, I already got in a half-mile! Same old stuff with me. Work's stressing me out as usual. But we always talk about my work woes—I need to hear about you and Liam. Is he still good with the situation with your mom? And have you met his daughter yet? What's her name again, Ellie?" Carla asked.

"It's Emma. Emma Lynn. She lives in Tennessee with her mom, so it's been hard to meet her besides talking online. You know how teenage girls are with a new stepmom. She hasn't been into visiting him lately, so that's why we haven't met. Spring break is around the corner, so she'll stay with him for about a week and then head back home. Hopefully, I can have lunch with her alone, and he'll bring her over one evening so we can mesh as a family. At least the online talks kind of broke the ice," Alexie replied.

"Well, it all sounds a bit weird to me. I think you need to ask more questions about why they divorced. You don't want to wind up in a bad situation. There's got to be more to it than what Liam told you. You went through enough with Kevin. You got a hair tie? I should've used more pins to keep my hair up."

"Well, he said they met young, and when he changed career paths, she kind of flipped out. Maybe she married him for the status or the money she thought he'd have. He was in school to be an attorney and realized it wasn't for him. He said she started seeking attention from other men with money and status. What's not to believe about it? And he's really good with my mom—better than I could hope for. We're working out details to make it work and avoid stress for both of us," Alexie said.

"You know how I am, Lex...just cautious. Maybe not because of what you went through, but because of what I went through too," Carla said, placing her hand on her heart while peeking from under her hat. "I know Liam is a good catch. Forgive my paranoia—and maybe I'm a little jealous!" They laughed as they passed the amphitheater.

"Guess what I got in the trunk? I need all my friends over to help dig holes and plant. It's that time again!" Alexie said.

"Another plant party! I...I can't. My back is still aching from the last one!" Carla said, bending over to rub her lower back with a playful smirk.

"Come on! It'll be fun like last time. All our backs hurt for days, but you know it was worth it!" Alexie said.

"You know I'll be there. You throw the best plant parties with old-school songs and that huge table of goodies. I've never seen anything like it! Your neighbors probably think we've lost our minds singing like the kids from *Little Orphan Annie*. But I'm doubling my fee this time—I need two bottles of wine! I'll bring a few things for the charcuterie," Carla said.

"Hate to change the subject, but you haven't mentioned your mom. How is she? And how are you?" Carla asked, stopping to look Alexie in the eyes, fully aware of the history between Alexie and Christine.

"We're okay," Alexie said, shrugging and pulling at the threads on the bottom of her shirt, breaking eye contact. "She's different and pleasant ninety percent of the time. So it's like having a stranger in the house who's my new mom, you know? It's a little weird, but I guess a good weird."

"I just don't want you stuffing or hiding what's going on, especially in your head. Call if you need to talk about the other ten percent when she reverts to her old self, or about your recent run-ins with Kevin. I hope he moves away—running into him so much can't be easy," Carla said.

"Well, I really need to figure out what I'm going to do about this other mother figure in my life! A true helicopter mom too!" Alexie said, giving Carla a side-eye and playful grin.

"Who, me?" Carla laughed. "How many plants this time?"

"Umm...lost count! I tried to just get a few and stay within budget, but you need to smell these tea olive bushes and the pretty pink bushes that bloom every two months! Yep, the whole car is full like last time. I let the windows down, so we're good for lunch and hanging out a bit."

They laughed as they crossed the small bridge over the creek and headed toward the large gazebo near the yellow-painted playhouse, retrieving their lunches from cold packs in their cars. Local moms and kids were scattered throughout the park. This was a perfect spot to brainstorm a few wedding plans with Carla and Renee.

They spotted Renee walking in from the farthest parking lot. She finally reached the picnic table. Renee was also a college friend, with a short, wavy curly haircut, fashionable sunglasses perched atop her head, tanned skin, and sparkling pink toes. She wore a pastel pink shirt and dark grey, work-appropriate pants. Deep dimples framed her brown eyes, and a large bag stuffed with wedding magazines hung from one elbow, while a half-eaten sandwich balanced in her hand.

"Hey y'all—hey! I only have an hour to get back to the office," she said as she made her way around the table with hugs. "I just wanted to get you started! I know you have lots going on and aren't ready to dive fully into planning yet. You were so excited before your mom moved in—you need to get that back!"

"You and Liam still good, right? What's your style? I see a modern farmhouse vibe! Y'all good? He still on board even with your mom? Catch me up to speed," Renee said, shoving the remainder of her sandwich into her mouth while digging in her bag. "I need more info. I need to know exactly what he said about your mom moving in," she added, still chewing. "Then we'll end on a positive note, getting closer to your wedding day!" She pulled out a small container of fruit while scrolling through an online wedding site on her phone.

Carla and Alexie exchanged a laugh at Renee's fast, no-nonsense approach—ready to tackle life and business all at once.

"What? Y'all know I talk a mile a minute. It's lunch break time. I ain't got long—you should've spilled the tea before I even sat down!" Renee said with a chuckle.

They spent an hour catching up on their lives. Alexie made a mental note to speak with Carla later, as she was less talkative about her job and herself overall. Alexie frequently glanced at her watch—it was almost time for her mother's sitter to leave. Her life now revolved around her sitter's schedule and her mother's budget. For a few hours, she had forgotten the challenges awaiting her.

She left Carla and Renee standing under the gazebo, still chatting, and snapped a photo of a beautiful flowering bush she hadn't seen before. Whenever she spotted an eye-catching plant, she photographed it to determine where it would fit in her yard—a form of therapy. The smell of tea olive bushes, the sound of wind chimes while reading among colorful blooms, the taste of her pesticide-free blueberries shared with friends in her backyard sanctuary—therapy.

Liam, now working a hybrid schedule from home, would meet her in the yard to help unload her plantings during his lunch break. He was already waiting in the driveway when she arrived. As soon as he spotted her car, he exited his vehicle, dressed for spring in a salmon-colored shirt, shorts, and sunglasses.

Liam was somewhat preoccupied—his aunt had recently died, leaving many details regarding her estate unresolved. She had no husband or children, and the family was already bickering over minor household items. Liam decided to step back for now, focusing instead on helping Alexie with her mom.

He walked to her car and opened the door.

"Is that a new perfume?" he asked.

"Nope! My new bushes. Grab the wagon and help me out!" Alexie said.

"Hey, I was wondering if you wanted to go to Greenville this summer. If we plan in advance, we could ask the sitter and pay her a little extra, and maybe Carla or Renee could stay with your mom while we're gone until we return that night. There's a food tour I want us to do if you're up for it. I already asked Renee, because I didn't want to get your hopes up and have it fall through if we didn't have a plan for your mom. I know you'd want it to be someone you trust. But if you don't want to, we can just cancel," Liam said.

Before Liam could finish, Alexie reached up and cupped his face, pressing her forehead to his with her eyes closed. "Thank you. I was just missing Greenville and wondering when we could go back with everything going on. I really need some time away!" she said, stepping back quickly.

They moved all the bushes and plants to the backyard and then sat together on the swing. The sun was still bright and warm. The flowering bushes and plantings attracted butterflies and several species of birds hiding near their nests. A pair of blue jays and cardinals flitted about, along with a family of hummingbirds—perfect motivation to buy a bird feeder. Alexie reconsidered the placement of her wind chimes, realizing they might scare the birds. Maybe she could find a better spot on the other side of the yard.

They sat in comfortable silence for a while, watching the bird activity. Inside, Christine rummaged through a bag in the family room as Melinda, the sitter, waved goodbye from the driveway. The cameras Liam had set up around the house provided an ideal angle to monitor Christine while allowing Alexie to enjoy yard work safely. She could also bring Christine onto the screened-in porch, keeping her secure while Alexie worked outside.

"So, Emma is still coming for spring break? I expected to meet her in person by now. I hope nothing gets in the way. Is her mom still good with it?" Alexie asked, pushing at the pea gravel beneath her feet.

"She doesn't have a choice but to be good with it. I told her I'd go to court again if I didn't see her soon. Between the two of them, it's been one excuse after another. Something's up with Emma, and maybe I can get her to talk about it while she's here. She used to love visiting, and lately, she's been avoiding calls and video chats. I'll get to the bottom of it soon. But if I have to go get her out of that house to bring her here... I will," Liam said, wringing his hands.

"Yeah... let me know how I can help. I also want to take her out, so maybe we can ask what activities she'd like to do when she gets here. Teens usually need time to adjust to having a stepmom. I know I might not be accepted right away. It'll be good for you to have quality father-daughter time," Alexie said.

"LEXIE!!" yelled Christine. "Who is that out there on the swing?"

"It's me and Liam, Ma! Remember I told you we'd be out here. You need something?" Lexie called back.

"We'd better check on her. I've been reading about dementia behavior. Maybe she's hungry and can't express it. I'll help you make her a quick lunch before heading back to work," Liam said as they went inside together.

After settling her mother, Alexie returned to the back porch with her laptop. Christine had fallen asleep in her recliner, often drifting off after pacing and rummaging through drawers—tiring herself out as the day went on. She was most confused in the evening. Alexie hoped this late-afternoon nap wouldn't lead to a late night of repeated questions. Every moment of peace for herself counted.

Liam left for the evening. While making a cup of pomegranate green tea and tidying the kitchen, Alexie found an old photo in a drawer. It showed her sitting on her bed in her childhood bedroom at about nine years old. She remembered the beige, bare walls—no pictures, no posters. Christine, still in despair at the time, had not decorated the room for her daughter.

Her childhood room had been a blank, drab spot in her life. She felt empty and isolated—no siblings, no close friends, just a few fleeting acquaintances. Christine never allowed friends over, so Alexie often sneaked to use the phone to call her cousins while her mother slept. Dinner was mostly frozen meals or peanut butter sandwiches—something to eat, but nothing enjoyable or home-cooked.

She had adequate clothes and warmth, but nothing special. Books became her refuge. Christine had to find ways to keep her distracted, to avoid giving her attention. Outside her bedroom window were beautiful trees, alive with birds. From that window, Alexie first developed her love of nature, longing to explore the world beyond it.

From then on, Alexie vowed that when she was older, her surroundings—both indoors and outdoors—would be vibrant and pleasant. She wanted seasonal colors to remind her of all that was good and right in the world. Placing the photo at the back of the drawer, she flipped it over. This was just one piece of her childhood she chose to shield from her memories.

"Mom, you're up. That was a short nap. I brought your dinner. Make sure you drink your juice this time," Lexie said, placing the dinner tray in front of Christine in the recliner.

Christine swatted Lexie's hand away as she set the tray down, almost knocking it off the table, startling Lexie.

"I don't want it! Get out of my sight. I hate looking at you. If it wasn't for you, he'd still be here! ...always asking to be picked up from school instead of riding the bus like all the other kids! GET OUT!!" Christine yelled.

"I'll be back later to make sure you eat," Lexie said robotically, trying not to react.

"Don't bother! I don't need you telling me to eat! Close the door!" Christine snapped, placing her wrinkled hand over her eyes and forehead.

Lexie closed the door and slid down the hallway wall, both hands covering her face, recalling the many times her mother had blamed her for her father's death. If she hadn't insisted on her dad picking her up from school, she would have ridden the bus, and he wouldn't have had the car crash. The overwhelming guilt she had learned to process returned like an unpredictable wave. She sat there for hours, reliving her mother's harshest attacks, before finally picking herself up and retreating to her room for the remainder of the night.

The next morning, Lexie turned the door handle slowly, trying not to make a sound, and cracked the door to peek in on her mom. Christine was already up, balling up her napkin and tossing it on her plate. Lexie opened the door halfway and stood in the doorway, head down, bracing for the next outburst.

"That sure was a mighty breakfast. More like dinner. Have you seen my purple bag? Come on in. Why so sad this morning? Look at how bright the sun is already. What's the matter, darling?" Christine said, concern in her eyes, having no memory of the previous night's confrontation.

"Nothing, Ma. You forgot to drink your juice. Let me get the tray and bring a fresh glass. This one's been here all night. Melinda will be by soon to help you get dressed," Lexie said, avoiding eye contact.

"Well, I don't know about that, dear. Who's Melinda? I just can't have any ole' body up in my house. Why can't you help me?" Christine asked, combing her hair with stiff, wrinkled fingers.

Lexie ignored her mother, picking up the remnants of the tray and leaving the room. She made herself a cup of coffee and sat by the window. The birds chirped faintly in the distance. The color in her front yard seemed muted today. Lexie watched Melinda walk past her rose bush onto the porch, dressed in sage-green scrubs with her hair in a braided bun, a large shoulder bag slung over her, and vibrant Crocs on her feet.

"Hey, Lexie! How's it going?" Melinda called.

"It's going. One of those days."

"You okay? You know she can't help it, and she doesn't mean it. She says the sassiest things sometimes. Don't let it get to you! It's the disease. You just have to let it roll off your back...like when someone disabled says stuff without understanding the impact. You give them a pass because they don't know better. I had to do the same with my Pop. He had it bad."

"Thanks... I guess that makes sense. But she was like this before dementia. How do you excuse that?" Lexie asked, wrapping her arms around herself as she gazed out at the backyard.

"Well...before dementia, it's different. Maybe that's just plain forgiveness, mercy, and understanding on your part," Melinda replied as she entered the room to greet Christine.

Lexie's phone buzzed. It was a text from her cousin Nicole:

"GM. I heard Aunt Chris was staying with you for a while. I wanted to check if you needed anything. Maybe I can drop off food or something to make it easier. I'll be checking on you both more often. Should return from my work trip by next Tuesday. Love you."

"Yes, thanks. We need to catch up. Hope everyone is well," Lexie replied.

Alexie focused on distracting herself from her conversation with Christine. She knew her mother had blamed her for her father's death as a coping mechanism, lashing out in grief—but it didn't erase the sting of decades of accusations. As a child and teenager, she had lived in a cloud of guilt, though as an adult she understood the circumstances were beyond anyone's control.

That night, Lexie asked Melinda to stay overnight in the guest room to help with her mother. Lying awake, she revisited some of her most painful childhood memories. After finally falling asleep and waking from a nightmare, she turned on her lamp and opened her drawer, seeing her journal, Bible, and sleep medication.

She reached for her journal and a pen. Writing had helped her in the past, but tonight she sketched landscape plans for her backyard. It was soothing and gave her something to look forward to. She penciled in loropetalums, rose bushes, tea olives, and spring and summer perennials. A few bare spots remained along the fence, needing another tree-like bush to mix with the others. She wanted a rotation of blooms—something always in flower. She had a couple more weeks to plant before South Carolina's summer heat.

The next few days were spent working hard in the yard: rolling out weed cloth, creating new planting beds, and preparing for her friends to come help plant. She avoided spending much time with her mother, wary of another outburst. There had been no sign of the old Christine for several days. Inside, Alexie had set up activity stations on the screened-in porch: rummaging bags, magazines, and textured distractions. Occasionally, while outside, she would call out to her mother to reminding her to drink.

After lunch, Alexie sat down with her laptop while Christine napped in her favorite recliner in her room. Alexie searched for local adult day care centers and eventually found herself looking at full-time dementia facilities. She hated thinking in that direction again but felt she needed to weigh her options. Her phone rang.

"Hey, Nicole. Did you get back from your work trip early? I thought you had a few more days," said Alexie.

"Yeah, I finished the training early. You've been quiet lately, so I wanted to check on you. I know what you've been dealing with. Only the family knows how Aunt Chris can lay into you. Has it been bad? How long are you gonna keep her?" asked Nicole.

"Well, most of the time she's like someone else—and even pleasant. But now and again *she* comes out for a few minutes. The hardest thing is not knowing when it's going to happen or how to get over it when it does. You know. You've seen her in action. It seems to be happening less often. I'm starting to feel guilty for being glad she has dementia. I don't think I could keep her if she didn't have it. I looked at full-time facilities today," said Alexie.

"Ya know nobody in the family would look down on you if you did. Sometimes you gotta do whatcha gotta do. The whole family saw her abuse whenever we got together for the holidays. Everybody felt sorry for you but didn't know what to do. I'm assuming it's why the family didn't come around often. At least there are places out there that would take care of her, but I bet it's pricey," said Nicole.

"It is. I'm hanging in there, hoping she'll keep this new personality and that more of her real personality will gradually disappear. There, I said it. It's a shame, but that's how I feel. She's my mom, and I wouldn't even consider taking care of her if I didn't believe she had some kind of breakdown when Dad died. Not excusing how she treated me. I'm trying to do the good Christian thing—'honor your mother'—and take care of her if I can. But I know that doesn't mean she has to live in my house, especially with these outbursts. We've got to figure out her finances and ours to see what we can do so I'm not tied to the house with her," said Alexie.

"So, you actually want to keep her if you can? That's surprising. She must've changed a lot. I gotta see this for myself. I'm coming down to hang out with y'all soon. Maybe I can sit with her while you and Liam go out, so you don't have to pay someone all the time. Speaking of Liam?" said Nicole.

"That would really help. We have medical and financial appointments for her soon, and I should find out what benefits and coverage she can get. If she stays pleasant, I can keep her as long as I have good breaks and time with Liam. He's been really good about all this. He knows when I need help and when I need space. But needing space won't work after we get married and are living in the same house. I've gotta find better ways to cope. So far, plant therapy is working! You coming to my planting party again?" said Alexie.

"Aaaah. Uuuum. Plant party? Again? You're sounding obsessed! I'll let you know. Or I'll throw a few in the ground when I come see Aunt Chris if I don't make the party. So, I'll see you soon," said Nicole while laughing.

Alexie sat on her new swing, strategically placed so she could admire her planting and yard work. Christine slept in her second-favorite recliner inside the screened-in porch. The birds took turns chirping almost in sync, with an occasional owl hoot. She'd been hearing the owl for some time but could never spot it. Maybe one day he would reveal himself. She secretly named him Hoot.

Alexie scanned the yard, trying to find the perfect spot for a bird feeder but still couldn't decide. For a moment, she even forgot Christine was there. It was almost time for Emma to visit Liam, and Alexie shifted her thoughts to connecting with her. She imagined taking her shopping at the mall, getting bubble tea, or maybe inviting her to the plant party.

Alexie's phone rang.

"So, where do you want to go tonight? I didn't get a chance to plan things the way I usually do. I was on the phone with Emma most of the day, and then there was my Aunt Barbara's estate. It's driving me insane. Do you feel like having steak, Mexican, or sushi?" said Liam.

"Tonight, I feel like a good sloppy burger. How about the burger spot in Chapin? They're always good, and we can get there before the crowd," said Alexie. "Maybe we can sit outside since it's kind of warm."

"Burgers it is!" Liam exclaimed.

They drove toward Chapin, making easy, pleasant conversation.

"So, I was thinking I could bring her over to meet you in person and let you two make plans from there." Liam glanced over at her. "You look tired tonight. You okay? I mean, you always look great, but tonight you look tired... like tired in your spirit," he said gently.

"I haven't slept well since... well, I was hoping not to talk about it tonight. I wanted to focus on positive things," she said, stirring her drink. "It's Mom. Most of the week was good, but we had one night where she went all the way back. And it wasn't good. I had a nightmare about Kevin that same night. When she's at her worst, it triggers the things I went through with him. I'm okay, though, and plant therapy helps a lot."

"Well, what about real therapy? You've been through a lot, and it wouldn't hurt to see if it helps. Therapy helped me after the divorce—processing the guilt I felt over being a horrible dad to Emma and leaving her with a troubled mother. Just think about it." He smiled softly. "But let's talk about happier things. I think I'm getting closer to that promotion I told you about. My boss asked me to meet next week. When you're done with your leave of absence, you may not have to work unless you want to—especially since you're caring for your mom. But no pressure. Do you miss it? You haven't talked much about your job since you've been on leave."

"Maybe because I haven't missed it much," said Alexie. "I miss my kids a little, but not the day-to-day bureaucracy of the medical field. The school system schedule is great. Weekends and holidays off—I used to think nothing could beat that. But you know what? There *is* a better schedule. I wouldn't mind going PRN. I could make my own hours and work only when I want to. I'd have the choice to say no. It's a good option now that Mom is in the picture."

"Well, you've worked long enough. You've earned the right to say no. If we hit the lottery or came into a lot of money, and you could do anything—paid or not—what would it be?" asked Liam.

"I don't know. I've thought about working at the nursery part time, just to learn more about plants. I feel so relaxed when I'm out there for hours. Maybe that's what I'd do," said Alexie.

"If that's what you want, I think you should try it. Maybe start with a few hours a week to test it out. I bet Tess would let you shadow her at the nursery on a day Melinda's watching your mom. You've got the best yard in the neighborhood. It looks professionally designed. You ever think about landscape design? You could do it—and make your own schedule. All it takes is a few good clients, and the referrals would follow," Liam said, leaning toward her with excitement.

"I never thought about landscape design. Maybe I *could* do it. Wow. You know me better than I know myself," said Alexie.

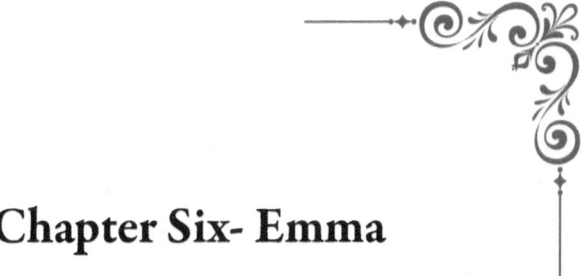

Chapter Six- Emma

They spent the rest of the evening talking about landscape design and planning their next Greenville trip. They agreed it might be a good idea to let Nicole stay with Christine while they were gone, since she was a familiar face and family to Christine. They ate good sloppy burgers with fried pickles, shared dessert, and opened their hearts about following their passions.

This was why Alexie decided to give Liam a chance. She loved how their conversations—first as friends—were real and positive. He gently told her what she needed to hear, yet she always left feeling lighter, supported, and believed in. And loved. It felt good to experience genuine love and admiration, though it still felt awkward to her. Alexie was learning to accept and trust that good things were finally happening. She was learning to trust that he truly loved her, while what she felt for him was almost too big to name. Sometimes it amazed her how easily they read each other and knew when to give space. Alexie decided to wait before asking about Emma's situation; he would talk when he was ready.

Alexie was both anxious and excited to meet Emma. She paused at the mirror before opening the door, took a deep breath, and smiled at herself.

"Heeey, Emma! So glad to meet you!" she said, giving Emma a hug. "So glad you're here!"

"Hi. Glad to meet you finally too," Emma replied, less enthusiastically, pulling back slightly.

Emma wore baggy jeans and an off-shoulder long-sleeved tee. Her wavy brown hair—just like Liam's—fell to her shoulders, gently tucked behind her ears. Alexie noticed Liam's demeanor was off. His smile was missing, and he looked concerned, while Emma seemed serious and nervous.

"My mother is in the other room with her sitter. Liam told you about her, right?" said Lexie.

"Yes ma'am, he did. I'll try to be kinda quiet," said Emma.

"Call me Lexie. And you don't have to be too quiet—she makes plenty of noise herself. You can meet her later. I made us lunch on the back porch," said Alexie.

As they walked toward the porch, Emma stepped outside and into the backyard. She stared for a moment, then slowly walked the perimeter, touching the plants and bushes, giving Alexie and Liam a few moments alone.

"Hey, are you okay? What's wrong?" Alexie whispered to Liam.

"I can't get into it now. We'll talk later. There's a lot going on with her, and she won't let me in. I'm worried. She barely talks, seems spacey, and she's lost a lot of weight. I just know something's wrong. You think she could be on somethin' or...?" he whispered while pacing inside the screened porch.

"Okay, don't panic. Remember, she's a teenager now and probably self-conscious about her appearance. You might be overreading it. Just give it a little time," Alexie whispered back.

Emma opened the screen door and peeked in.

"Can we eat out here on the picnic table? It feels like a park back here. This is really nice. Can I hang up my hammock later?" said Emma.

"Yeah, sure. Can you help me bring the food to the table? So, what grade are you in now? Any plans for after high school? And I love your shirt," said Lexie as they walked out together, with Liam trailing cautiously behind them.

Lexie and Emma enjoyed light "getting-to-know-you" small talk while Liam watched their interactions curiously. At the end of the evening, Emma surprised Lexie by initiating a hug. Then she turned to Liam, signaling she was ready to go, her expression relaxed and upbeat. Liam looked back at Lexie and shrugged behind Emma.

"You are amazing. Thank you," he whispered as he hugged her goodbye.

"Bye, Lexie. See you tomorrow! Love your house and the yard! Come on, Dad!" said Emma, skipping lightly toward the car.

They backed out of the driveway, and Liam's smile had returned.

"Thanks for staying late, Melinda. Having an extra person in the house really throws Mom off. I really appreciate it. I'll give you a bonus," said Lexie.

"Mr. Liam already took care of that. I just have one request," said Melinda.

"Let me get a cutting of one of your plants. I've been eyeing it for a minute! Oh—and Ms. Christine is already asleep. I gave her some Sleepy-Time tea, and she was tuckered out from our walk earlier. It shouldn't interfere with any of her meds—I checked," Melinda added.

"Oh sure! Take whatever you want! Thanks for always looking after Mom in the best way. I don't worry about her at all when you're around," said Alexie.

"No problem. You know my pop and my late husband had it, so it's quite familiar to me. I think I mentioned that to you a bit ago. It's late, so I'll get the clipping later in the week. She seemed to take to you well. I think she's looking forward to you being in her life. Seems she's craving female attention and connection—just my two cents," said Melinda, speaking of Emma as she slipped one arm into her sweater.

"Yeah. It went better than I thought. Thanks again!" said Alexie as she helped her with the other arm.

Later that night, Liam called Alexie to thank her again for figuring out how to connect with Emma.

"Hey, Lexie, you worked magic with her today. I mean, I feel she is still off, but she's a little bit happier, and she talked about you and your place all the way home. She came out and sat on the couch, and we watched TV after. I would've liked to talk to her more, but at least we sat in the same room without it being awkward," said Liam.

"I was just trying to get in her space a little and not make it all about me. Ya know, Melinda mentioned she felt Emma was craving attention—like real female attention. Melinda is usually right when she reads folk."

"Well, I doubt she's getting any of that from Lisa. She's always out with some man, and leaving Emma by herself in the evenings is what she's told me. That's probably half the problem. I can never get her mother to pick up the phone," Liam said.

"Hopefully she'll want to spend more time with us later. Maybe we can get her to spend the summer here next year. I'm looking forward to it. I've been cleaning out closet space for you. I got rid of a lot of stuff I ain't worn in ages."

"The house is looking great. And I can't blame her for wanting to hang out in the backyard. I admit I can't wait to leave my place. After we get married, I'll be moving into the best spot in town! Hey, you said you didn't want to talk about it on our date. What was your nightmare with Kevin about? I'm only asking because it's been a while since you had one. I figure this thing with your mom is triggering it."

Alexie was silent as she sat on the couch, scribbling circles in her journal.

"Never mind. I just thought it might help if you talked about it. But if talking takes you back, then I'm sorry I made you think about it."

"It was a nightmare about the day you put a stop to it all and me and Kevin broke up. But it was a nightmare because he came back looking for you and threatened you, and he was in the house throwing things around. The same recurring nightmare I had when I first left," said Lexie.

"Well, we have nothing to worry about. That's just the devil trying to destroy your new peace. That chapter in your life is over. Eventually it will be over your mind, too. That's my prayer. We still meeting with Pastor Mark for our pre-marital counseling after church Sunday?"

"Yeah. Save me a seat in church. I promised Carla I would pick her up, and I need to check on her. I was gonna call, but I need to see her face to face. She seems a bit off. Well, you'd better go since it's getting late. I'll text when I'm on the way to pick up Emma for bubble tea tomorrow. Love ya, bye!" said Alexie.

Lexie hung up and continued to scribble circles and patterns in her journal. She wanted to write words, but circles and patterns were all she could muster.

Her mind drifted back to the dream. Back to the day she decided to be done with Kevin.

They had been dating for more than a year, and Kevin frequently talked of marriage. Alexie desperately wanted to be married. Who doesn't want to be loved and taken care of until the end of life? Kevin told her he wanted her to quit her job, insisting there was no need to work since he'd be taking care of her. He frequently pressured her to turn in her notice, but she wasn't ready. She liked her job at that time, and she loved her two best friends from work. She looked forward to going in. She soon realized she was searching for spaces and reasons to escape Kevin's control and criticism. Work had become that space—with Liam and Deidre.

He looked down on her job since it didn't compare to his two-hundred-thousand-dollar salary. He was jealous of her friends and constantly tried to get her to stop attending church services—another source of peace and joy for her. Their values didn't match. But he was so charming and promising in the beginning. She fell for him, thinking he would learn to love her values. She was blissfully, hopefully blinded by his empty promises.

Liam and Deidre were her work buddies, counselors, therapists, and fun in her life. She told them almost everything. Almost. Except for the extent of Kevin's verbal attacks. He was constantly condescending, convincing her she was starting to look old and that nobody but him wanted her.

Liam and Deidre were trying to lift her up spiritually and emotionally after Kevin told her she had better quit her job by Friday or they were over. His nickname for her was "Crows Feet," and he addressed her as such in their text messages, thinking it was comical. She had finally gathered the courage to show them the texts and the awful nicknames he used for her. "Crows Feet" was even the contact name he assigned her in his phone. She felt so relieved to finally discuss it with someone. She remembered the details of that day like it was yesterday.

Alexie and Kevin were at a restaurant when he grabbed her phone and scrolled through, reading the communication between the three work buddies about his own subtle abuse. He tossed her phone onto the dinner table.

"Let's go back to your place. I'm not hungry anymore. We need to have a serious talk," Kevin said to Alexie with a cold, stern face, disapproval oozing from his demeanor.

"Well, why can't we talk here? It's not crowded and I'm hungry," said Alexie, going with her gut not to be alone with Kevin.

He had never hit her before, but his aggressive tones and snide remarks cut like a knife. She wondered if this would be the time. The time he'd lose it. The time he might... He had grown to hate Deidre and Liam and saw them both as competition. He wasn't the guy she had first met or the one he promised to be. Her gut told her to let him calm down a bit before going back to her place.

"We can talk after we eat. It makes no sense to get here and just leave. I want the burger with guac," said Alexie nervously as she picked up the menu.

"I'm going to ask to get our food to go. And the last thing you need is another burger. I'm getting you the salad. Meet me at the car," Kevin retorted, getting up and slamming his menu on the table.

While Kevin was at the counter ordering, she texted Deidre and Liam and told them she feared what he might do after seeing their text strand. She sent the text and shoved her phone back into her bag before Kevin returned. It was also before she could see their response.

As they were driving back to her house, Kevin started yelling and raving to the point spit flew from his mouth. He was yelling so loud he didn't hear her phone going off in her bag as Liam and Deidre took turns trying to call, desperate to know if she was safe. Kevin drove erratically all the way to her house—sometimes in the middle of the road, weaving in and out of traffic, insinuating he would make them wreck without saying it. He was a master at those sorts of threats.

As he pulled up to the curb, her phone rang, and he snatched her purse, digging for her phone while Alexie got out and ran toward her house. She stopped and collapsed to the ground in relief when she saw Liam's car. Liam, Deidre, and Deidre's husband Bryan were parked in her driveway, standing outside... waiting.

Liam walked toward Alexie to help her up, and Kevin threw open the car door and ran toward her.

Alexie stood, and Liam stepped in front of her with his arm out, keeping her behind him and out of Kevin's reach.

"Nope... we're not doing this. Not today. Not ever. YOU need to leave," Liam said, peering into Kevin's eyes, breathing deep and steady, refusing to break eye contact.

Kevin walked up to Liam with both fists clenched, staring into his eyes. For a moment, they seemed to breathe in sync. Then Kevin took a step back. Deidre and Bryan were walking over, and Deidre yelled that she had called the police.

"It's over. We are done!" said Alexie through tears from behind Liam's shoulder.

Kevin walked swiftly back to his car, started the engine, rolled down his window, and shouted, "ALL y'all can have her! I am the one who's done!" He sped off before the police arrived, throwing her phone and purse out of the window.

They all slept over in the living room of Lexie's place that night to make sure he didn't return. Alexie filed a police report, and Liam installed cameras around her house the next day. She recalled the fear mixed with relief as Liam rescued her that night.

Lexie had placed her journal on her bed and was now squeezing her pillow tightly as all of her emotion rushed back, recalling the night as if it were yesterday—holding the pillow the same way she held on to Liam's arm in the yard. It was a horrible night, but also the night that changed the trajectory of her and Liam's friendship to a level she didn't know she could experience.

She picked up her journal and wrote. She wrote seven pages. Then she slept deeply, with no nightmares, having let it all spill onto the pages of her journal.

Chapter Seven- Bubble Tea Date

Alexie made her way to the back porch a bit early the next day. She felt slightly refreshed from a good night's sleep and sat on the swing, watching the cardinal couple dart in and out of the bush. She thought of the perfect spot to place the bird feeder—right outside her mother's window. Christine often sat in the recliner with the blinds raised. Maybe the birds would bring her the same calm Alexie felt from watching them in her own childhood.

Alexie waved goodbye to Liam as she left to pick up Emma for bubble tea. Emma was even friendlier this time. They placed their order, and Alexie sat down to wait for her. Emma wore leggings and a loose, long-sleeved blue shirt. As Emma sat, she lifted her right arm to tuck her hair behind her ear, and her sleeve slid to her elbow. Alexie noticed four two-inch scars, perfectly lined up on Emma's arm. When Emma saw her looking, she tugged the sleeve back down and dropped her head. Alexie gently lifted the sleeve again and touched her arm.

"Emma? Are you cutting? You can talk to me—tell me what's going on. Are you thinking about hurting yourself?"

"Don't tell Dad! I just have a lot of stuff going on in my head sometimes," she whispered, pulling her sleeve back down and crossing her arms over her chest.

"How are things with your mom? Can you talk to her? Does she know?"

"No! I don't talk to my mom. Just promise me you won't tell Dad! He's already worried enough!"

"He cares about you. I can't promise I won't tell him, because I care about you too. Why don't we pick a time, and we can both sit down and tell him—just so you can get the help you need? Is there something you're trying to distract yourself from? I know how that is... we want to help and protect you," Alexie said gently.

"Well, he cares, but he's not there for me. He's here with you while I'm stuck in that hellhole with my so-called mother!" Emma snapped, her voice hardened, her arms crossed tightly, her eyes filling with tears she refused to release.

"Hey... let's go somewhere more private and talk. Or we can just walk. I always talk better when I walk. Is that okay with you?"

"Yeah, I guess," Emma mumbled.

They left for the park and walked for an hour and a half. Afterward, they drove back to Alexie's house. Melinda and Christine were far out back near the rose bushes, about to plant marigolds in the new beds Alexie had made. Inside, Alexie led Emma to the guest room. Despite her tear-swollen eyes, Emma lit up when she saw the room Alexie had prepared. It wasn't big, but it was clean and soft—colored pillows, candles, everything she needed to settle. Alexie had even stocked books on the shelf and added a small chaise for music listening or reading, with soft blankets folded neatly nearby.

Exhausted from sharing her story, Emma crawled under the warm covers fully clothed and buried herself in the big pillows. Alexie pulled the blinds and told her she'd check in often but wouldn't wake her. As she turned to leave, she saw Emma toss her leggings and shirt onto the floor beneath the covers. She closed the door softly.

Alexie walked back to the kitchen and sat at the table, touching the edge of her blue tray positioned carefully in the center. She pondered the bits and pieces of the broken life Emma had tried to express in such a short time. She understood her. Doing whatever it took to distract yourself—running, burying yourself in something, or even inflicting pain.

She wondered whether the pain of cutting distracted from other painful memories or served as a reminder that you were still here when you felt numb, bare, invisible, and empty. She knew that feeling all too well. As a teenager, she'd shared similar thoughts once. She planned to wait until closer to Emma's drop-off time and ask Liam to drive over to talk. Alexie drifted into memory again.

Many years ago—Alexie was almost seventeen.

She peered out the screen door on the front porch, waiting for the daily mail. Beyond the green grass and sporadic tall oaks were the cornfields she gazed at daily, searching for movement, life, anything. Ms. Shelby's house sat at the edge of her cornfield off to the side, where she gave the occasional wave.

The mail car slowed along the grass, inching toward the mailbox. That was Alexie's cue to head toward the one-lane highway frequently traveled by what she called the Big Mack trucks. She eased the door open quietly so her mom wouldn't yell out and remind her how fast the trucks traveled or to look both ways.

No shoes in the heat of summer in the Carolinas. Careful steps across sprouted grass bursting through the hot black asphalt, hopping over the tiny ant piles scattered along the way. She had to cross the road quickly before her mom could spot her from the window. What was she thinking, going barefoot in the heavy humidity of early June? The heat stung the bottoms of her feet, forcing her to hop a little faster. The daily mail drop had become an event in the monotony of her long, idle days.

After looking both ways, she crossed quickly to the silver mailbox. She flipped through the envelopes—nothing interesting or important. The usual junk mail addressed to her mother. She turned to cross again, eyes still on the stack of mail. She took two steps, hesitating to look at the meal coupons tucked inside. In that instant, she felt a car door graze the outer shirt she wore over her halter top. She froze as a white blur sped past, carelessly racing down the highway without slowing, without consideration for anyone crossing. No horn. No engine sound. Just a rush of air, a ruffle of her shirt, and a flash of white.

Alexie burned with anger at the thought of almost being hit right in front of her house—for her mother to find. Saved by a two-second pause. Then another thought flickered: what if she *had* been hit? Would that be so terrible? Maybe she wouldn't be so miserable in whatever afterlife waited. She wished she hadn't paused. Wished she had stepped out just a moment sooner.

She recovered from her thoughts quickly, clinging to the determination to leave her mother's house as soon as she could—awaiting college, new friends, and pleasantries. She brushed it off as a fleeting moment where death felt easier than life. Alexie decided there was still more life ahead, more that could get better. She just needed distance. And she would make that happen. She only had to hold on a little longer. And she did. And life *was* better. Alexie shook off the memory and started planting a few seedlings on her back porch.

Alexie let Emma sleep for a while before knocking on the guest room door.

"Hey, feeling a little better? Rested? Do you want to go with me to the plant nursery? I need to figure out those empty spaces where the neighbors can look straight in on us," Alexie said.

"Sure. I do feel a little better." She pulled the covers to her neck. "Let me get dressed," she added, waiting for Alexie to step out so she wouldn't see more scarring.

"Okay. I just need to snap a few pics to show Tess. She'll know what to put in those bare spots," Alexie said. "I need you to help me find a small bird feeder, a birdhouse, and maybe a wind chime to go way out back by the roses near the bench. Let me know if you see anything you think will look good in the yard."

They walked into the nursery, and Emma went to browse through the items Alexie wanted. Alexie spotted Tess, stooped low as usual, reaching for something for a customer.

"Hey, lady! Who you got with you today?"

"Hey there, Tess! My fiancé's daughter—my soon-to-be stepdaughter. What kind of bush or small tree can grow fast enough to fill these spots?" she asked, pointing to pictures on her phone. "Something evergreen. I need a few plantings that will grow quickly, or maybe some already on the way up if they're not too pricey."

"That's a job for a Wax Myrtle bush. It gets big like a tree but looks like a bush right now, so make sure you give it room. Over yonder, in the back corner. Come on," Tess said, briskly heading off over yonder, her off-white, slightly dirty apron flapping behind her.

"This smells like the bush in your yard!" Emma called from a few rows over.

"Yep—the heavenly scented tea olive bush! That's the one," Alexie said.

They drove back, and Alexie helped Emma set up her travel hammock in a shady spot between the pines in the backyard. Emma seemed content—water bottle, a sleeve of peanut butter cookies, and a book in tow—as she lay in the hammock with one leg out, swaying gently. As Alexie walked back toward the house, she heard Emma chattering to a friend from Tennessee. Alexie kept a close eye on her until they could talk to Liam.

"Hey, I was calling to tell you I need you to come over here instead of me dropping Emma off at your place," Alexie told Liam.

"Why? Is everything alright?"

"Yeah, it's okay, but she wants to talk to you and tell you something. You were right—she has a lot going on."

"Like what? What's wrong? Why are you holding back? Just tell me what's going on!" Liam said anxiously.

"She made me promise not to tell you. But I told her I'd help her tell you when you got here. She's going to be okay. I don't want to start off wrong by breaking her trust. Can you just come over? You'll find out soon enough. She's out back in her hammock. I promise she's okay at the moment."

"At the moment? I'm on my way. She texted and asked me to pick up food so you wouldn't have to cook. She said y'all were busy with girl stuff all day. She sounded like it was a normal day."

"That's probably not a bad idea, picking up food. And maybe it *was* a good day for her—getting things out in the open, off her chest. I'll see you soon."

Melinda and Christine had made their way back inside. Christine headed to her recliner while Melinda entered the kitchen to make tea.

"Melinda, how long did you have to do this with your family? You said your husband and your dad?" Alexie asked.

"Total combined, it was about twelve years overlapping. But I had help with my dad from three siblings. We rotated him until we couldn't do it no more and he went bedridden. Then we put him in a facility and made sure we visited a lot. You don't have that kinda sibling help. So you gotta be more creative, and there may come a time when you—"

"I know," said Alexie.

"It'll be alright. Gotta treat folk the way you wanna be treated if you were in their shoes. That's what the Lord says. Good things come to ya if you do it His way," said Melinda in her deep Southern accent as she stirred honey into her cup.

"Yeah...not always easy. And we went through four people before you, trying to find someone who would treat her right and that I trust in my house. I caught one lady rambling through my things in my room, maybe looking for something to steal. Just want you to know you are deeply appreciated," she said, looking sincerely at Melinda while pouring herself a cup of tea.

As she walked back into the family room, Emma had found her way inside and was conversing with Christine. Emma had poured out a puzzle and started helping Christine piece it together. Lexie stopped, a bit startled.

"Y'all alright?" said Lexie.

"Yeah!" Emma walked toward Lexie and whispered, "I think she thinks I am you when you were young. She was talking about all kinds of stuff and trying to apologize to me—or I guess really to you—about somethin' from years ago."

"Apologize about what? She thought you were me? She didn't try to hit you or anything, did she? I'm sorry if she said something awful to you," said Alexie with alarm as she walked over to the coffee table.

"No. She just said there was something she should've told you long ago about your dad, and she was really sorry. I think she got distracted when you came in. I tried to keep it going when you were walking in so you could hear. I'm gonna finish this puzzle with her before Dad gets here. Is that ok?"

"Yeah, sure!"

Alexie grabbed a big pillow from the couch and sat on the floor beside Christine. Her mom had never attempted to apologize for anything in Alexie's life. What could she possibly have to say about her dad that Alexie didn't already know? The anxiety rose in her chest.

"Mom, were you trying to tell me something earlier?" Alexie asked, hoping Christine would slide back into the conversation.

"Did you make me some tea, dear? I was talking to Lexie earlier," Christine said as she played with the fringes on the decorative shawl in her lap. "What's your name again? You got the prettiest eyes!" she added, looking out the window at the birds in flight to the bird feeder.

"What were you apologizing to Alexie for earlier?" asked Alexie, realizing Christine didn't recognize her.

"I don't know. Stuff from long ago. We can talk about it later. Where's my tea? I saw the cutest birds and flowers outside in the park today!"

Alexie hoped Christine would finish her earlier confession, but only dementia spoke when she questioned Christine. She gave up for the moment and decided to enjoy the new version of Christine for the rest of the day, though she couldn't shake the curiosity. This she needed to know.

Liam pulled into the driveway. Melinda was leaving, and Christine was fast asleep in her recliner. As soon as Liam arrived, Emma tore into the bags and dug out her burrito bowl.

Liam was ready to talk but pushed through dinner to avoid Emma shutting down.

Alexie joined Emma on the porch as she finished her bowl.

"You ready? I'm sure it'll go well. Let's get it over with," said Alexie.

"I guess," Emma said, walking into the kitchen and picking her nails anxiously.

Liam sat silently, tapping his foot with his hands clasped. Alexie had never seen him like this.

"Do you have something you want to tell me?" he asked Emma as Alexie moved closer to her for support.

"Dad, Mom has been gone a LOT! She's been leaving me for days and sometimes weeks on end while she travels and does stuff with boyfriends. Some of them are real creeps... Dad... She told me not to say nothing or I'd get put in foster care if folk found out how much she leaves me alone. Most of the time I'm by myself or home when all these men come looking for her when she's out." Emma put her hands on her face and sobbed.

"How long has this been going on? Has anybody hurt you?" Liam asked, his body tensing as he fought to steady himself.

"She's been doing this since I was little. Since you two separated. For years. Alexie felt I should tell you that sometimes...I cut myself with a razor... just to relieve stress though... I'm not gonna hurt myself."

"What? Are you okay? Do I need to take you to the hospital? How do I know you won't hurt yourself? I just want to make sure... put your shoes on so we can go," he said as he stood up.

"Dad, no! I'm not going to the hospital. I don't feel like I want to hurt myself right now." She turned and looked at Lexie. "I told you this is how he would react. Please don't take me to the hospital. Can't I just stay with you for a while? Over the summer? I just need a break from it all. Maybe you can convince Mom?"

Liam looked toward the ceiling and sighed deeply, trying to contain himself. He got up and hugged Emma. "You can stay at my place over the summer and probably forever if I have any say in it. I'll deal with your mother later. You sure you don't need to go to the hospital? If you don't go to the hospital, you have to be in therapy over the summer. It's your only option."

Emma sat silently for a minute, wiping her face with the tissue Alexie had given her.

"Okay... I just didn't want to go to foster care, or I woulda told you, Dad. It's been a lot."

"You will never go to foster care as long as I'm alive. She told you that to scare you into staying silent. You didn't know, and it's not your fault. I'll deal with Lisa later," he said as he hugged her and walked to the doorway to go outside—then turned around and came back to Emma.

"Is there anything else, Emm? Did anyone... hurt you... in any other way?" Liam asked softly.

"No, Dad... not really... I fought them off. There were a lot of creeps trying stuff when she wasn't around. There are things you don't know about Mom. She has huge issues! It's okay. I would tell you... Can I go to the guest room for a bit? Dad, can I stay over with Lexie and help her with the plant party tomorrow?" said Emma, shifting to another subject.

"Yeah, as long as it's okay with Lexie," he said, his back turned as he wiped away tears.

Emma went to the guest room. Liam stood in the kitchen doorway with his hands in his pockets, staring at the floor with tears in his eyes. Alexie was still sitting at the kitchen table.

"You should've called me. I still think she should go to the hospital to be evaluated," Liam said, his eyes on the floor as he tried to contain his anger toward Alexie.

"I've been watching her since she told me. I was trying to do this without causing her more trauma. If I'd felt she would've hurt herself, I would've called and taken her myself," said Alexie. "I think she'll be okay if she's taken out of her present atmosphere. And I will call to set up counseling for her. She just needs to be somewhere other than Tennessee with Lisa right now."

"How can you be so sure she won't hurt herself?" said Liam.

"I don't know for sure. But I feel she won't. I'll help keep a close eye on her. She seems really happy to be here. She needs a change of scenery and new people to be around, ya know? I think we can give her something to look forward to. The worst is over. Now she just has to deal with her memories."

"I should've known better than to leave her with Lisa and trust she... and I don't believe nobody never hurt her. How can a little girl fight off grown men all the time? It just doesn't sound realistic," said Liam.

Alexie came over and hugged Liam in the doorway.

"You can't blame yourself. She's gonna be okay now that you know. Let's just focus on what she needs in the moment. If she's been through more, she'll tell you when she's ready—or maybe it'll come out in therapy. She may have repressed memories. For now, you just have to trust what she's saying until she's ready. You can deal with Lisa later, and I think she'll thrive staying with you this summer. She'll be a new girl!"

"I hope so. Thanks for getting her to open up. I didn't mean to be... I'm sorry for how I came across."

"Let's go to the swing and decompress a bit. Try some chamomile tea. When Melinda comes back, I'll go with y'all to help her decorate your spare room and get what she needs. We can talk to the school and get her to finish her classes online. It's only one quarter."

"Yeah, and at least I won't have to worry about her anymore and she'll be safe here. I can't even think about the conversation I'm about to have with Lisa! I think I need something stronger than chamomile tea!" he smirked, leftover tears still at bay as he ran his fingers through his hair and shook his head.

"Let's go for a quick walk. Mom is sleeping pretty hard, and I told Emm to call us if anything came up. She was listening to music in her room and on the phone with one of her friends from school. She's okay. And maybe you should wait to have that conversation with Lisa so she won't contact Emm about telling. Give Emm a few more days without the drama. We can just circle the block and come back. Ya know, she kind of had a connection with Ma. Kinda surprising. She wasn't nervous around her and was actually helpful."

They walked the block a couple of times to decompress from the day.

Chapter Eight- Plant Party Day

Alexie kept her bushes and plantings watered and sunned until the big day—Plant Party Day. It was a day she created a couple of years ago when it was safer to be outside with friends than indoors. She'd inspired a circle of friends to plant flowers, create beds of beauty, and start healthy home-grown food. She saved the bigger tree plantings for Liam or the nursery guy she hired for the heavy work she couldn't lift on her own. She had already placed all the plants in front of the spots where they would be planted.

Today's landscape lineup included tea olive bushes, pink and red fringe loropetalum bushes, a variety of rose bushes, marigolds, and snapdragons. She had prepped and staged multiple shovels and lawn tools.

In front of the plants were new pairs of yard gloves, hand shovels, big soft blue floppy wide-brim yard hats, and cool water cups—one for each participant. Inside the back porch, a table covered with a yellow-and-white plaid tablecloth was pushed against the wall, filled with jams, spreads, honey, figs, deviled eggs, sliced meats, assorted nuts, berries, dark-chocolate-covered pretzels, fruit, and much more.

Alexie and Emma had prepared bread-and-butter pickles, gherkins, bruschetta, and several specialty cheeses sprinkled across the table, along with Alexie's famous homemade chicken salad scooped into halved coconut shells. Not an inch of the six-foot table was without a grazing item, each section piled high and plentiful.

Emma thought it looked like artwork—the most beautiful grazing table she had ever seen. And of course, there was homemade raspberry lemonade punch, stirred with a rosemary stem, and several bottles of wine for guests to enjoy and take home. Alexie couldn't wait for her newly planted fig and peach trees to bear fruit so she could create new jam combinations. She had recently learned to make tomato jam—a specialty she served on top of fried green tomatoes and homemade pimento cheese with fresh greens. It was her favorite appetizer at the hotel she visited whenever she went to Savannah. She'd created her own tomato jam recipe, and it was worthy enough to sell.

Liam assigned himself to the grill. All the girls usually showed up with a special dish or two. Within the raised beds she planned to grow cilantro, peppers, tomatoes, green beans, cucumbers, and eggplants. She'd also recently learned how to cultivate sprouted red potatoes from her kitchen—soon to yield several pounds with a little dirt-hilling and patience. That would be enough for now; seeds and starters were organized and ready to go. She'd see what the stores restocked each week, but she needed everything planted before the heat set in. She'd learned that the hard way one year.

Emma stepped into the screened porch and scanned the table from left to right.

"I can't believe we did this! What did you say this was called?" she said, wide-eyed, picking a grape and pulling out her phone to record.

"It's called a grazing table. Or a super huge charcuterie board. You can put whatever you want on it. The more stuff, the better," said Lexie, grabbing a pair of clippers from the side table. "See that bush in the corner? Can you cut me several sprigs to dress up the table a bit? We'll tuck them in around the edges underneath. It's due for a trim," she said, pointing to the rosemary bush closest to the porch.

"Which one again? Rosemary? What does it look like?"

Alexie stepped inside, grabbed one of the sprigs she had drying on a napkin in a basket, and brought it out to Emma.

"It looks and smells like this. One touch and the scent will stay on your fingers," she said, placing the small piece of rosemary near Emma's nose as Emma pulled back slightly.

"Wow! That's strong. Okay...I got it," Emma said, dashing off the porch with the cutters and sprig in hand.

"Hey! Slow down! Not a great idea to run with scissors!" yelled Liam, now standing in the doorway, looking at Alexie with reassurance and quiet pride.

Alexie smiled and whispered, "See? Natural therapy."

Cars began pulling up along the curb. Music played while hollers of "It's so good to see you!" filled the air. The smell of burgers and brats drifted from the grill as Liam worked. A car pulled into the driveway and caught Alexie's attention. She waited to see who would step out.

"Deidre! I didn't know you'd be in town! Hey Bryan! Y'all come on in!" Alexie shrieked.

"Well, Liam told Bryan what y'all were doing, and we decided to surprise you and drive in. We'll stay at my sister's for the weekend and see family, but I had to stop in for Planting Day," said Deidre, handing Bryan a grocery bag for the grill.

"Hey Bryan! Liam's out back!" Alexie said as they exchanged quick hugs.

Another car pulled up, and Alexie squinted over the line of parked cars to see who else had arrived. The door swung open, and Alexie recognized Tess climbing out, still wearing her tan apron and carrying a few extra plants.

"Hey Tess. I'm glad you made it. We need somebody to tell us what not to plant where and such! Thanks for the extra," said Alexie.

"I can't believe I've never been to one of these!" Tess said as she headed into the backyard. "Girl, you ain't playin'! Wow! Look at all this! Hey, y'all!" She threw her hand up and waved to everyone.

Tess made her way to the grazing table and mingled with the crowd. A few people stood in front of the spread, taking pictures and video of the charcuterie display. Bryan and Liam were at the grill, adding what they called "more sustenance" to the menu as they walked past the table grazing together, calling it "heavy snacks."

They laughed as Liam handed Bryan a big soft blue floppy hat, which Bryan quickly plopped back onto Liam's head. Emma seemed to be enjoying recording the event and helping Alexie with the new activities. As the grazing and planting got underway, the old-school playlist brought on a wave of singing. Neighbors drove by slowly, trying to figure out what was happening. Some nodded and waved in approval; some stared curiously; and only a couple cringed at the parking pileup.

Alexie noticed the top of a straw hat moving back and forth on the other side of her fence. Anna was one of the quiet, not-so-friendly neighbors. Alexie had tried to have her over before, but Anna always seemed aloof and dismissive. Alexie made her way toward the hat, remembering a recent sermon about loving your neighbor as yourself. As she got closer, she saw Anna's eye peering through the fence slats. Anna darted away the moment Alexie approached.

"Anna! Hey there. Just wanted you to know the noise won't be long. It's my yearly spring planting party. How old is your niece who lives with you? I know you don't want to cook tonight...we've got so much food. Grab your niece and come eat and meet my friends," Alexie said, thinking it would be good for Emma to have someone her age over.

"Umm... I actually love to cook," Anna said proudly, lifting her chin. "But Leslie could use somebody to hang out with. We'll just stay a little bit. What can I bring?"

"Really nothing. I don't want to have all these leftovers, so please come help us eat this stuff! See you in a few minutes," Alexie said, surprised that Anna had agreed.

Anna had been peering through the fence cracks for a couple of years and was partially the reason Alexie had searched for evergreens for privacy. She arrived a few minutes later with Leslie, who held a plant, gloves, and a bowl of freshly made salsa. Anna had been dying to get into Alexie's yard to see what she had been working on. Her eyes traveled from east to west as she took in the festivities and the personalities—though with caution. Leslie found Emma, and the two settled onto the swing, sharing videos on their phones.

As the sunlight faded, the new string lights flickered on with a warm glow over the picnic table and garden, creating the firefly-like ambience Alexie wanted. She thought it was a perfect day. The lights reminded her of evenings at her grandmother's house, running barefoot with her cousins, determined to catch fireflies in jars. Those were her best childhood memories. She missed her grandmother—her warmth, her gentle spirit, her famous tuna salad sandwiches, macaroni spaghetti, homemade biscuits, and something fried and tangy she called tripe.

Alexie found ways to pull those memories into her home décor. She had created a large firefly using a wooden table leg for the body, ceiling fan shades for wings, wire, nails, and colorful spring paint for the rest. It looked almost like a dragonfly, but it was the best she could make. The firefly-dragonfly hung on the porch wall and was often a conversation piece. She always told guests about chasing fireflies at dusk with her cousins at Grandma's house.

The singing died down as guests left, grabbing their favorite bottle of wine from the table. "Until next year!" they said, taking home paper goodie bags from the grazing table and leaving Alexie with minimal cleanup. She noticed Bryan and Liam deep in conversation near the back fence—no doubt Liam was filling him in on the new concerns about Emma. Alexie was glad Bryan was there when Liam needed a listening ear.

Melinda had taken Christine out for dinner and a long walk, tiring her out before bedtime. Melinda knew all the tricks. Christine fell asleep as soon as they returned. Alexie made Melinda a generous plate of the day's food to take home. The noise and commotion would have frustrated Christine, who struggled to remember who people were, so Melinda arranged an outing—and Liam paid her a bonus for it.

Deidre and Alexie planned to catch up privately over lunch the next day after church. Emma asked to spend one more night with Alexie before returning to Liam's place. Alexie surprised her by hanging a set of string lights across the guest room wall and ceiling. When Emma walked in, her eyes lit up almost as brightly as the lights. Alexie wanted her to have a space that felt welcoming and age-appropriate—something she herself had longed for as a child.

Alexie's cheeks were sore from smiling all day. She kept replaying how good the day had been. After she and Emma finished the light cleanup, Alexie ran a deep tub of bathwater, lit candles around the room, and called Emma in, handing her a towel and a glass of raspberry punch. Emma held back tears; no one had ever been so attentive to her needs. She closed the door and slipped into the bath.

Alexie sat in her room, pulled out her journal, and wrote about the day. She overheard Emma humming a song. She felt Emma was becoming the little sister she never had.

Chapter Nine- Sunday Morning

The next morning, Alexie rose from her sleep screaming, "Dad, wait!" as she sat upright in bed. She recalled dreaming of her father running through the woods in his favorite tan plaid shirt, just ten feet ahead of her. She could hear herself crying in the dream, unable to catch him, and he wouldn't look back until he fell to his knees and yelled for her not to come closer—to go away. She covered her face with both hands as she sat in bed. She wondered if the smell of the barbeque grill yesterday had triggered the nightmarish memory of him. He always smelled of barbeque smoke.

She had been looking forward to Sunday—church and time with people—but the dream had taken the wind out of her morning. Alexie had grown to love being around folks, though sometimes after a large gathering she needed to retreat and recharge so she'd have something to give later. She texted Carla and asked her to find a ride since she no longer felt she could make it to church.

Today she didn't feel like the strong, coping version of herself. At least for the morning, she stayed in bed. Liam had only texted to give her the space she needed and let her know he'd come by later to check on her and pick up Emma. Alexie turned her phone face-down on the nightstand and rolled over.

It wasn't until later that she heard pots clattering in the kitchen. Emma was supposed to be sleeping in, and Melinda had taken Christine to church and then to lunch. She threw on an oversized sweatshirt and sweatpants and walked into the kitchen.

"I was just making you some tea for when you got up... Emma let me in. Are you alright?" said Liam.

"I'm okay. I just didn't feel like I could make the service today. I'm feeling a little more drained than usual after everyone was over. I needed a break to process things. I'll go next Sunday. I didn't want to miss our session with the pastor, but I started feeling kind of depleted, ya know? Maybe it was too much after the party yesterday. How was church?" asked Alexie.

"It was really good. Carla asked about you. I left a little early to check on you," Liam said, pouring a cup of tea for them both. "Emm is in the shower. I'll go ahead and take her early so you can get some time alone before Christine gets back."

Emma came out of the bathroom to grab a bag for a few of her things. "Hey, Alexie... are you okay? I thought I heard you talking in your sleep this morning. Also—is something wrong with the toilet? Is it not flushing? It seemed fine when I tried, but I asked because someone didn't flush it last night. I was scared I might make it flood!" she said, wide-eyed and curious.

Alexie looked down at the floor, embarrassed. "I think it's okay. Sometimes I just forget to flush. There are more bags in the pantry if you need one for your things," she said, trying to redirect and distract.

Liam looked at Alexie with warmth and concern. She knew what he was thinking—therapy would help all of this. She stirred wild honey into her tea and tried to shift the conversation before it started. Emma returned to the guest room.

"You've missed church only twice this year—once when you had the flu and once after the nightmares about Kevin. Are you sure you're okay?" Liam asked.

"I just needed to sleep in. Just tired from yesterday... but what if I'm not quite okay? Am I allowed to have a bad morning? I need to be allowed to have one or two now and then," she said, frustration creeping into her voice as she turned slightly away and sipped her tea.

"You're allowed to have as many as you need—especially after taking on your mom. I'm just trying to figure out how to be here for you. I want to help; I just don't always know how."

"I'll be okay. It's just a lot at once. I'm sorry for snappin' at ya."

"Call me later when you're ready to talk... I mean, if. I'm going to take Emma to the house. We'll call Lisa together to figure out next steps for her," Liam said as he gave Alexie a quick side hug. "Call me if you need anything. I already ordered lunch for you. It'll be dropped off soon."

There it was again—that warm safe feeling. Something she couldn't quite explain with Liam, but it was overwhelmingly good.

She called Deidre and traded their lunch plans for dinner. Deidre and Bryan always brought a smile to her spirit. She hated when they moved, but they were always just a call, a text, and a couple of hours away from hanging out. Liam and Bryan had been college roommates and stayed close for years. Deidre always reminded Liam that after marriage they were a package deal. Liam and Alexie welcomed that package. They'd sit for hours playing cards, having wine with dinner, and discussing bucket-list short trips with food tours. Soon they were joining several couples on a

Greenville day trip with a scheduled food tour—something they all looked forward to.

Alexie had to fight to keep these things in her life now that her mom was in the picture. She decided she had to find a way to make it all work, regardless of what life threw at her. And now there was Emma. Alexie had been wondering what would eventually happen to Emm. She was willing to do whatever it took to make sure Emma was safe. How could she do any less after Liam had been so accommodating with her mom?

She hadn't anticipated a teenage daughter in the mix of her life, but she welcomed the challenge.

When Bryan and Deidre were in town visiting family, they would have lunch after church and discuss the message and church happenings. Folks had a hard time transitioning back to church after 2020, but life was getting back to normal, and the seats were filling up again. People were trying to ease back into the rhythm of life—back from being online to the socialization everyone had missed. Alexie and Liam were both naturally introverted.

On the introvert scale, Alexie was a six and Liam about a four. She figured gravitating toward being outgoing was another form of therapy. People were a good distraction from piercing memories. Positive new moments with others helped push the old ones back. People, hobbies, and perspective mix with faith came with time and created peace. Alexie could use the distraction from her memories.

The dreams were harder—deeply embedded in her subconscious, rearing their ugly heads unexpectedly. She hadn't yet mastered them. Sometimes she told Liam; sometimes she didn't. She felt they were like the whack-a-mole game: knock down one nightmare about Kevin and another disturbing dream about her deceased dad would pop up. But she'd figure it out, just as she did everything else. She shifted from the slow, heavy morning into a better afternoon and looked forward to hanging out with Deidre and Bryan.

Before the couple arrived, Alexie called Carla. She had been meaning to check on her and had Carla on her heart.

"Hey, Carla. I'm sorry I couldn't make it this morning. It was one of those rare mornings. How was church?"

"No problem. We all have those days. It was great. He spoke about forgiving people and the past... and showing mercy to folks who may not deserve it. I'm sure they recorded it," said Carla.

"Sounds like something I probably needed to hear. I'll check it out later on the website. Hey... are you okay? You seemed different last time we walked. Less talkative about work. Less talkative about what was going on with you."

"Well... I was less talkative about my job stress because I no longer have it. I quit my job, and I didn't want to tell you right away. I didn't want you to think I couldn't handle my wedding responsibilities. I have pretty good savings... so I'm still doing my Maid of Honor duties."

"I can't believe you finally quit. But I'm glad you did. The level of stress it caused—and how it affected your health—was too much. There are so many jobs out there where you'll be appreciated."

"Yeah, I feel at peace about it. I'm going to take the summer off to figure out my next steps. I don't want to rush into anything out of fear and end up in the same predicament. But I need you to promise me something. Promise you won't take away my Maid of Honor duties! I know how you think—always putting others above yourself. Really, I can handle it. I've been much better since my grandmother's inheritance last year. It put me in a place where I could quit and not worry. I was going to tell you... eventually."

"Okay... I promise I won't take your duties away. I have so much going on, I sometimes forget I'm getting married in six months! Well... I need you to promise you won't hide any more of life's biggest events from me," said Alexie.

"Deal."

They caught up about Emma and more while on the phone. They planned to walk again across Lake Murray Dam soon.

Deidre and Bryan arrived in their usual fun mood. They ate at the picnic table, lights glowing above, playlist playing. Alexie felt Liam was more relaxed after talking with Bryan about what was going on with Emma. Bryan was fun but also grounding—always reminding you that things tend to work themselves out. He and Deidre were perfect for each other. Not flawless, but perfect for each other. A few months earlier, Deidre had confided in Alexie about the rifts they were working through in their marriage. But at least they were working through them, not giving up. You'd never know anything was wrong when you saw them together; they always appeared to be the perfect couple in public.

Alexie was glad they were working through their issues. She needed them to be okay, since they were a friendship package. She planned to hang out with Deidre next month to check in and make sure they really were OK. She realized she had been doing a lot of that lately—checking on folks to make sure they were okay. She gave others what she needed most: someone to make sure she was okay. She was thankful for friends like them. A rarity, she thought.

Liam, Deidre, and Bryan left for the day. Melinda had made Christine's dinner and set her up at the table.

Melinda glanced at Alexie, then walked toward the sink so Christine couldn't hear. "Are you going to eat with your mom today? Seems like you've been eating most days in your room while she eats at the table. I'm sure she'd appreciate your company."

Alexie gave Melinda a blank stare. "Oh yeah. I'll eat with her tonight. I just have a lot on my mind."

"You know caretakers can't replace daughters. I know you and your mom have been through a lot. But if you've decided she should live with you, you may as well... be here... you know," said Melinda. "Gotta be understanding and let go of the past. Mothers have so many regrets they can't take back when they age. They really want to take back all the hurt they caused."

"I know. I also know she's different and ailing now. It doesn't make dealing with the memories any easier," said Alexie, pushing the edge of her kitchen rug with her toes.

"I had a really hard childhood too. Things I can't talk to nobody about. I learned from the good book that forgiveness is also for me. It's freeing. It doesn't give anybody the right to treat you bad, and sometimes folks need boundaries; it just makes it easier to move on. I sure hope nobody holds my sins over my head the rest of my life — even the really bad ones. You know where it says forgive your brother seventy-seven times, or ten times over in so many words. Well, they may not sin against you that many times, but you may remember it that many times, and every time you do, you have to decide to forgive in the moment of the memory and move on. There is no excuse for bad treatment. But people do change and regret what they've done and the pain they've caused. Even if they don't change or regret it... bitterness don't kill nobody but you. The best revenge for bad treatment from folks is to process it, forgive it, and leave it in its proper place... behind you. 'Cause

God doesn't treat us as our sins deserve. So, we don't treat others as their sins deserve. Right? Amen! Just thought I'd share the message from church with you today!" said Melinda as she lifted one hand toward the Lord.

"Amen," Alexie said, holding her head down and nodding. "Yes ma'am. Sounds like I missed a good message I need to listen to later. I know she was deflecting a lot of pain. I figured that out as I got older. That's a lot to think about. My body is here, but not my heart. Daughtering from a distance even in the same house. Thanks for showing me myself, Melinda," said Alexie.

"You know there are many ways to take care of elderly folk. As long as you see to it that they're taken care of, it don't have to be done by you if it ain't possible. Kind of like when kids are young and moms want to be stay-at-home moms but they need to work and don't have family who can watch 'em full time. So they take their young'uns to the best day care they can afford, run by folks they trust, and they pop in often to make sure they doin' right. It's the same sometimes with aging parents if it gets to be too much. Pray 'bout what you need to do, Love."

Melinda left for the evening, and Alexie decided she would help her mom get to bed. Her mom usually slept hard on Sunday nights after all the extra walking and activities. Alexie decided to run to the store to get a few items she needed for the pantry. Christine was sound asleep. She could be back in twenty minutes and still see Christine from the cameras. She thought again how some of the same cameras that were put up to protect her from Kevin were also watching over her mom. Alexie headed to the store on a mission to get only five items and get back quickly.

She passed by the greeting cards and remembered Mother's Day would be here soon. Waiting until the last minute to search through picked-over cards was agonizing. She decided to go ahead and grab one while she was out. Searching for a card for her mother was always a challenge. Most daughters would spend a few minutes picking out a loving card describing memories of childhood and a relationship filled with care. Not so with Alexie.

She went through card after card looking for the right words. A card showing gratitude for being nurtured and cared for was just a lie for Alexie. Fake. That's not us. Next... Next... Nope, not that one. Card after card gushed with feelings of closeness and kind memories. Why hasn't someone created a Mother's Day card that just says, *I wish you well today and maybe thanks for giving birth to me.* She couldn't find a card that suited what she felt. Some gratitude for feeding and clothing her without all the positive memory stuff or the *you are an awesome mother* line. She gave up on the card hunt for now since she had little time and headed to the toilet paper aisle.

She stepped onto the edge of the shelving to bump the toilet paper toward the front where she could reach it. Suddenly someone taller than her picked up the toilet paper and held it out to her. Kevin. He held onto the end of the paper as she reached to take it from him.

"Can we get together and talk?" said Kevin, finally letting go of the toilet paper.

"Talk about what? We have nothing to talk about. I gotta go," said Alexie, feeling her heart rate increase.

Kevin grabbed her by the elbow as she tried to walk off, and she felt the hard pinch in her arm. Alexie forcefully snatched her arm away, startling him. "Get off me! Don't touch me! THIS is why we will never have anything to talk about!" said Alexie.

She left him standing in the aisle. This time she wasn't going to run out of the store. She needed her items and she was going to stay until she had all five things she came for. She gathered everything and walked to the register, seething with anger as the cashier rang up her items. The cashier peeked at Alexie over the top of her glasses, sensing her defensive fury, but she dared not speak to Alexie.

Alexie got all her items and marched toward her car. *How dare he touch me,* she thought! This time she would file assault charges. She slung her bags into the back seat and quickly got in as her cell phone alarm went off. She locked the doors, checked her phone, and saw her mom exiting the front door of the house in her gown, barefoot, on the home camera.

This can't be happening, she thought. She was only seven minutes away. She could get home before her mom got too far from the house. She remembered she had forgotten to put her mother's location tracker bracelet back on after her shower. She had to get home. She went to put her car in reverse and looked into the rear-view mirror.

Kevin had pulled his car directly behind hers in the parking lot and wasn't moving. She started digging in her purse to distract and act as if she didn't see him, waiting for the car to pass so she could pull out. Kevin's car didn't budge. Finally, she looked up in the rear-view mirror. Her eyes locked with his. His eyes were full of aggressive arrogance; hers full of anger and disgust. She stared him down with both hands gripping the steering wheel. She put the car in reverse with her eyes still locked on his. He held steady and revved his engine.

After a few seconds he smirked and sped off so she could finally back out of the parking space. Alexie backed out quickly, heading home to gather her mother. How ironic, she thought. Trapped by Kevin and the circumstances of her mother. She stuffed the incident into the back of her mind to focus on Christine. It was getting dark.

Her eyes scanned the sidewalks and the sides of the road as she drove home, searching for any sign that her mom had made it that far down the street. She didn't see Christine walking on the way back from the store. Where could she have gone?

Alexie threw her car into park, slammed the door open, and ran toward the backyard, leaving the groceries in the car. Christine was nowhere in sight. She hurried back toward the front yard, calling out her mother's name frantically.

Her neighbor Anna opened her front door and stepped onto the porch, looking out into the yard. Alexie ran toward her.

"Have you seen my mom? I saw her leaving the house on camera. I left her asleep in bed, and I was only going to be gone a few minutes!"

"It's okay. I've got her. She's in my kitchen having dessert. I was just about to text you, but it took me a few minutes to wrangle her from the sidewalk and convince her to come inside. She kept saying her baby was crying and she needed to find him. You know, I don't think it's a good idea to leave her alone even for a few minutes," Anna said.

"Oh, thank God. I thought I'd have to call the police to search for her. You're right. I shouldn't have left her. She's never tried to leave the house before," Alexie said.

"When they get like this, it's like having a two-year-old. You gotta watch 'em every second. She's been enjoying my lemon meringue pie, though—kept her distracted and kept her from leaving. It's like she's searching for something or someone. I gave her a pair of my slippers," Anna added.

"Thanks so much. I'll take her now. It won't happen again. But thank you for keeping an eye out. I may not have found her if you hadn't spotted her on the sidewalk. Come on, Mom. Let's go home. Thanks again," Alexie said as she guided Christine toward the door.

It took nearly fifteen minutes to coax Christine back next door; she was in such a confused state. And it was another hour before she finally stopped rummaging through drawers and closets and settled down for bed. Alexie collapsed onto the couch, exhausted from the double ordeal.

She debated whether to tell Liam she had run into Kevin once again—twice this month now. She didn't want to keep avoiding him, but maybe it was time to start shopping somewhere else. Or maybe not. Maybe she was tired of running and needed to confront him and tell him to leave her alone. She rubbed the sore spot—now a bruise—on the inside of her elbow where he had grabbed her.

She was too exhausted to think about Kevin or the extra level of care her mom needed. Almost around-the-clock supervision. ID and address bracelet with a tracker. A bedroom door alarm. Would she ever get a good night's sleep again, always on edge waiting for an alarm to go off? One-on-one care with Melinda was already getting expensive just for a few days a week. How could they manage it full-time?

Alexie kept replaying her conversation with Melinda about her mom. She knew she hadn't given Christine her whole heart or attention since she'd moved back—only ensuring her physical needs were met. She wasn't focused on conversation or meeting her mother's social or emotional needs, especially since her own needs had been stifled as a child. She was exhausted just thinking about how to be emotionally attentive to her mother while also trying to avoid Kevin. It was all too much. She pulled a blanket over her head and fell asleep on the couch.

The next morning, she woke to find Christine sitting across from her in the living room, flipping through a magazine. Her expression was stiff and stern. The old Christine was visiting for a moment. Alexie sat up.

"Mom, how did you sleep last night? I'll get us breakfast in a minute."

"No need. I'm not hungry. I already ate." Christine flipped another page in the magazine. "Your dad may want some," she said.

"Dad? Mom... you know Dad passed away a long time ago," Alexie said softly.

"What? When did that happen? Nobody told me! What happened to him? Nobody told me!" Christine cried hysterically, forgetting he had died as if hearing it for the first time.

Alexie tried to comfort her, wishing she had just said he was at the store and would be back later. Christine was reacting as though she was learning of her husband's death anew. She had truly forgotten. Alexie hated seeing her mother relive the grief all over again.

She helped Christine back to bed.

"I'm sorry, Lexie. I lied to you all those years. Please forgive me," Christine sobbed.

"Sorry for what, Mom? You haven't told me what you're sorry about. What is it you need to tell me?" Alexie asked, sliding down to the floor and resting against the bed beside her.

"You know what I said all them years about your dad. It wasn't right. It wasn't the truth. I didn't treat you right. Can you forgive me?"

"I forgive you, Mom. Get some sleep." Alexie closed the blinds and went back to the living room.

Her mom had said a lot to her over the years. So which of all the horrible things did she now regret? Maybe she was apologizing for all of it. But it seemed Christine was trying to communicate something specific about her dad. Alexie was puzzled, unable to make sense of it. Today wasn't a good day to try. She'd had enough emotional upheaval for the entire week. She couldn't handle another roller-coaster moment. She let the conversation go.

Chapter Ten- Dahlias, Dirt and Whispers

Weeks passed, and the old Christine showed up less often. Alexie had increased Melinda's hours a bit, and her cousin Nicole was able to sit with Christine once a week for about two hours. The cost was eating through all of Christine's Social Security payments and was on track to drain her retirement over time. Alexie was covering Christine's food and daily care items from her own budget. Every part of her mother's care had to be meticulously planned while Alexie attempted to plan her wedding. She was considering postponing it for three months just to give them time to adjust to both Christine—and now Emma.

While running errands, Alexie drove past a nursery she had never visited before. She almost veered off the road, staring too long at the gorgeous bright red and deep orange flowers with yellow highlights blooming near the roadside. She turned around to take a closer look. When she entered the nursery, she was greeted by Corrine, the Master Gardener, and the owner, Ms. Helen, both offering a warm smile and hello. This was the true hospitality the area was known for—helpful, friendly, inviting folks. Good people to all people.

Corrine took her time explaining how to care for the beautiful new dahlia plants and gave Alexie a complete tour of the nursery.

For a moment, Alexie put aside her worries about her mother. She decided to be fully present as she learned from Corrine about lemongrass tea and cultivating a healthy garden. Between Tessa and Corrine, she would have the healthiest yard around. She couldn't wait to get home and plant her new dahlias—and she couldn't wait to return to the nursery for more gardening conversation with Corrine and Ms. Helen. She also remembered she needed to stop by the Ballentine Library, which gave out free gardening seeds every year. Another warm, friendly place in town.

The garden was coming along nicely; everything had taken root and taken off, displaying bright colors and blooms in rotation. She planted the dahlias in the perfect spot for viewing. She spent some time weeding. The sun was bright and peeked through the small holes in the front of her coral sunhat. She noticed one tomato plant with dried leaves near the base, so she pruned it and worked a small amount of fertilizer into the soil near the pepper plants.

It seemed the plants grew at night while the world slept. Every morning, she would find new growth—stems strong and sturdy, stretching up and outward toward the sun like a child reaching for a parent to lift them. She loved the new long-handled waterspout Liam had bought her, which allowed precise control of the water stream. She had lost track of time and was watering her hanging baskets on the front porch when a gentleman pulled up in an aged light-teal truck and stepped out.

"Hello! Sorry to bother you. Can I ask you a quick question about your yard? I'm Nathan, your neighbor down the street."

"Sure, I'm Alexie. What can I help you with?" she replied cautiously.

"Do you mind tellin' me who's your gardener or landscape designer? I've been driving by your house for a while. Even before you put your fence up, I could see into your backyard. The Mrs. and I are retiring and downsizing, but we're movin' to a place with a bigger backyard, and she wants a landscape similar to what you've got," Nathan said, scratching his long white beard.

"Well, that would be me. I don't have a designer. I got a little help from the local nursery on Highway Six about plant care, and I did the rest myself—with help from friends for the heavier work. But I guess you could say I did the design."

"Is that right? So how much?" he asked in the deepest Southern drawl.

"How much? You mean how much I spent on the yard? Well, let's see..." she said, trying to do quick math in her head.

"No ma'am. I mean how much would you charge to design the landscape plan for me and the Mrs.? We just need the design after you see the yard. We'll do the work ourselves, and my sons will help. We're not so good with the vision part and could use some guidance. Like a consultation and a planting map after... Here's my number. If you can come see the new property and give me a price, we'd appreciate it. My wife will be present," he said, leaning toward her with a business card.

Nathan climbed back into his truck, waved, and drove down the street. Alexie stood on the porch, speechless, the business card still in her hand. She couldn't believe it. She had to call Liam.

Liam agreed to go with her, and she could always get Tessa's input on plant selection. He told her it was the beginning of what God had intended for her all along. Maybe he was right. She loved learning about plant care, but she loved designing her yard around her daily activities even more. The raw dirt and plant scents were intoxicating, relaxing, and energizing all at once. Maybe it was time to enroll in an online horticulture and landscape design class.

She could create designs from home using software, stay with Christine, and schedule consultations on the days Melinda was there. It was perfect. She could even volunteer or work part-time one day a week at a nursery to speed up her learning curve. The conversation she'd once had with Liam had now come into fruition. Alexie made dinner plans to celebrate her new career option and business.

Alexie thought she would use this time to discuss pushing back the wedding date with Liam. She felt they needed time to adjust, plan, and re-budget the wedding.

The server delivered two large burgers piled high with onion straws to the table.

"Hey. What do you think about our wedding date with everything going on with Mom, Emma, and everything else?"

"I've been wanting to see how you felt about it. We've barely had time to discuss plans and details, and I'm getting ready to take Lisa to court for Emma. How are you feeling about Emma living with us for a while—or maybe even permanently after the wedding? Instant family."

"Kind of the same way you felt about Mom living with us. Your family is my family. It won't be easy, but with a plan, we can make it work. I'm glad we're getting to know each other, and she and I bonded during the short time she was at the house. She feels like my little sister, but I hadn't thought of myself as a stepmom. Still, I don't want her going back into a neglectful and abusive atmosphere when she could be here with us. It makes no sense. It's a no-brainer for me. But I do wish we could push back the wedding date a little—just to give us more adjustment and planning time. What do you think?"

"I'm good with that. Why don't we set a date about three months later than the original? Just so neither of us is stressed. We have the rest of our lives—so what's three months?" Liam said.

"I think three extra months is good. I already feel less stressed just thinking about it. Carla and Renee may have something to say—especially Renee. She loves being on schedule. But they know what we've been dealing with. And really, what's three more months? We plan to be together for a whole lifetime, like you said. How did it go with Lisa?"

"She was irate. But she calmed down when I reminded her what court would be like for Emm. She knows the judge would award me full custody. That will eventually happen, but for now I don't want Emma going back—not for her immediate well-being. Emma's been off ever since we had the conversation with Lisa. I took her phone for a bit to monitor the crazy texts Lisa kept sending. She didn't stop until I told her I'd use the messages in court to prove she was unfit. Emma relaxed once the phone was out of reach. She wants to be here with us. This will give her more time to adjust."

Alexie heard a familiar laugh from the booth behind them. Her body stiffened as she looked at Liam. But this time she stiffened with determination—not fear. She was tired of running and hiding as if she were an outlaw. Liam clearly recognized the laugh too. He was facing the booth and could see it was Kevin—and that he was sitting with a slender blonde woman.

Alexie felt a small sense of relief that he was with someone else. She also felt the urge to warn the young woman about what she was in for. But mostly she felt grateful—him being with someone else meant he had finally moved on. Maybe he had gotten the message during their last encounter. She hadn't told Liam about the elbow grab in the store aisle.

"We can leave if you want and get our food to go," said Liam.

"Nope. I'm tired of cutting life short every time I run into him. Maybe I need to show him he doesn't rattle me—unlike last time," Alexie said.

"Last time?" Liam leaned forward, placing his napkin on the table. "What happened last time?"

Alexie told him about the store encounter when Kevin grabbed her by the elbow. Liam grew quiet and still. A few minutes later, the blonde woman left for the restroom. Without warning, Liam stood, walked to their booth, and slid into her empty seat to confront Kevin.

Alexie's eyes widened as she strained to hear their whispered conversation. What was Liam saying? Soon she could only hear Liam's voice—an intense, almost loud whisper—punctuated by a sharp finger tapping the table. Kevin said nothing and grew pale. Liam finished and returned to their table before the blonde woman came back.

"What are you doing? What did you say?" Alexie whispered.

"I told him not to ever touch you again or we'd put a restraining order on him—along with a few other things. He got the message, I think. And I don't believe he's with that woman romantically. Looks like a work dinner. They had papers all over the table. But I let him know he needs to move on and stop trying to engage with you," Liam said, settling back confidently in his chair.

"I wish you had told me you were going to do all that. I wasn't prepared..." Alexie said.

"Prepared? That's the point. You shouldn't have to be prepared. If he touches you again, we'll file a restraining order. It's the only way to show him you're serious. Someone needs to teach him boundaries. Actually, he's had enough chances. I think you should file the restraining order regardless—just to teach him a lesson."

Kevin and the blonde woman walked past their table as they left. Kevin didn't acknowledge them or look in their direction, walking swiftly out the door.

"Let him leave early for a change. So—interesting night so far! How's your burger?" Liam asked.

They laughed. "This may be the best burger I've ever had!" Alexie said.

There it was again—that feeling. Warmth. Safety. Protection. Liam was considerate and handled his business as usual. Alexie looked forward to a marriage with him as soon as life stopped getting in the way. They talked and celebrated her first landscaping consultation as they finished their food. They dreamed together about her new passion and the doorway into a new career doing what she loved. They talked about wedding details, and she felt no fear of the future.

They also talked about his upcoming promotion, and Liam vented a little about the stressful details of his aunt's estate.

They laughed again about Liam's intense whispering at Kevin and how people had started to stare. They talked about local restaurant-hopping with friends and everything under the sun. They also talked briefly about how they both needed to fight to forgive Kevin and Lisa, even with the intense interactions that continued. But they both understood the need to maintain strict boundaries regardless of forgiveness. They discussed the new book-club reading at church and the recent sermons that had hit close to their internal struggles.

Alexie felt relaxed and carefree. She felt loved—no anxiety at all. It was as if Kevin had never existed. She smiled through their long dinner together; another evening that left her cheeks sore. Sore cheeks from smiling were becoming a regular thing in her life, and it felt invigorating.

Liam dropped Alexie off at home. As she entered the house, she saw papers and things on the floor—everything looked slightly disheveled. For a moment she thought Kevin had made his way to her house in anger. She slipped her hand into her purse to grab her phone when she heard her mother's voice.

Christine was in the kitchen, throwing things out of a drawer. Alexie remembered the first of the Five R's for dementia care: *Remain calm.*

"Hey, Mom, what are you doing? What are you looking for so I can help you find it?" she asked gently, taking Christine's hand and guiding her to the couch.

"I'll be out in a second!" Melinda shouted from the bathroom as she flushed the toilet.

"I'm looking for the key. You know, the key to your dad's truck. He won't go to the store for me, so I'm going myself. The baby needs diapers!" Christine said as she patted the couch cushions in search of the key, lost in her dementia. Alexie dared not remind her mother of her father's passing after her last spiraling reaction, completely forgetting he had passed.

"Mom, you know we sold the truck a while ago. One of us will take you to the store tomorrow. It's late. Let's make a short list of what you need, and then let me help you back to bed," Alexie said, guiding her to her room with a notepad in hand.

Melinda quickly helped straighten up the mess in the kitchen before leaving for the evening. Alexie sat at the table, staring at her blue, intricately carved serving tray.

She drifted again into memory. Lexie was about five years old.

"Lex, bring the tray for the burgers! They're almost done!" her father called.

Lexie skipped to the kitchen and grabbed the blue tray her dad had carved himself, painted in her favorite shade of blue. It was her tea tray and sometimes doubled as the barbecue tray when she and her dad grilled together. He swooped her up with one arm and held her on his hip, away from the grill, while flipping the burgers onto the tray with the other hand.

He smelled of smoke—she called it *burger smoke*. They always tasted the first burger together, cutting it in half. Their secret. "Test-tasting," he called it. You had to make sure it tasted good and was done. She held tightly to his shoulder. She felt safe, warm, and protected. Kind of like when Liam was around.

Alexie smiled at the pleasant thoughts and the fond memories of her father before his passing.

Chapter Eleven-
Mother's Day

Weeks passed. Christine's behavior remained much the same—sporadically erratic. There were good and great days, and then there were the other days and nights. Alexie was learning a new pace with realistic expectations for her mom, which helped her set expectations for her own new life. She still wavered between sticking this out at home and exploring some form of respite-facility care. She prayed for guidance and became better at being fully engaged with her mom on certain days. The recurring nightmare of her chasing her father, hearing her own cries echo behind him, still appeared now and again.

Would she ever catch her mom on a lucid enough day—one where she might finally reveal what she had been hiding about her dad all those years? Now and again Alexie would try to ask, but dementia usually answered for her mother. She knew she would need patience until the truth surfaced, if it ever did.

Alexie made her way back to the greeting-card aisle. Only a couple of days left—now was the time to sort through and find the right Mother's Day card. She had picked up six cards, all with some version of "what a great childhood you gave me." None of them described their relationship. She decided to be a little merciful this year in her card selection.

She chose to look for the good and focus on the endearing moments of her youngest years—before her mother had been overtaken by grief and despair. She finally found a card that reached far back, describing the times of being lifted into her mother's arms, well fed, and tucked tightly into bed with bedtime stories...before Dad died, she thought. She'd better purchase it before she changed her mind or drifted into her teenage memories, the ones she desperately wanted to forget.

Flowers were easier. Celebrating your mother as though she were the best mom in the world—not so easy. But she had learned to process her mother's trauma, in a way. Could she herself ever be so consumed by grief that she would neglect and abuse her only child? Never. But this was where mercy came in. Alexie promised herself that if she ever had a child, she would not imitate her own mother's love; she would love differently. She decided she would show mercy to people who didn't deserve it. After all, that was partly the definition of mercy—treatment that is undeserved. She could do that.

She felt she had learned something from attending church these last few years—something she could actually practice, much like loving your neighbor as yourself. Again, she chose to give what she had so desperately needed at one point in her life. She chose to give mercy to the one she had once needed mercy from. So she bought the not-so-deserving Mother's Day card and was okay with it.

She decided to invite her cousin Nicole, her aunt, and a few others over for a Mother's Day brunch after church—to avoid awkwardness and create some healthy distraction. In the past, it had always been a day to simply get through. This time Alexie would celebrate who her mom *could* have been if not tormented by tragedy and grief. She decided to be thankful that she had food, clothing, and a roof over her head as a child, and let that gratitude soften the bitterness that surfaced when she remembered the other times. She had a few scars, she thought. But she never had broken bones or burns. Someone out there had gone through far worse.

This way of thinking helped her process everything. She was grateful that her mother's personality was now repressed into something gentler most days, making the present more bearable while she cared for her. She would enjoy her aunt, her family and friends, and the mother figures and mentors from church she now had in her life. She chose to enjoy whatever good was present in her mother that day—in the present moment. Not thinking about the past or too far ahead. She felt a weight lift from her heart, at least for now.

Melinda had become a wise presence in her life, prompting a new thought process for Alexie. She was both a mentor and Christian counselor to Alexie. Melinda deserved the day off for Mother's Day, too. Alexie decided she would manage without her that day and be fine—and she spoke it into existence.

The day finally arrived. Everything went smoothly as they attended the early-morning church service. Alexie spotted Melinda across the sanctuary sitting with her daughter. They exchanged a quick nod and warm wave. Melinda watched and nodded in approval as Alexie sat beside her mother. The service was blessedly brief. Alexie and Christine slipped out a little early to prepare for the guests.

Alexie set the table with a yellow plaid tablecloth while her mother sat on the porch bird-watching and quietly picking at a ball of yarn in her hands. Alexie arranged the chicken salad, pimento cheese, her homemade raspberry-rosemary lemonade, and a few other dishes she had prepared. The doorbell rang. On her way to the door, she darted into the bathroom to make sure the toilet had been flushed before company arrived. She smiled with relief at the clean and clear toilet bowl.

Nicole and her family were ushered in. As they were about to sit down to eat, the doorbell rang again—unexpectedly.

Alexie made her way to the door. Standing there was a stout woman with brown hair, bright eyes, and a warm, close-mouthed smile—just like Liam's. Behind her stood Liam and Emma. Janice grabbed both of Alexie's arms with warmth, pulled her into a hug, and gave her a cheeky kiss. As they embraced, Alexie glanced over her future mother-in-law's shoulder into Liam's eyes and whispered, "Thank you."

And there it was again—that feeling.

He anticipated what she needed at the most difficult times. Alexie noticed that his mother had an extra bag on her arm. Liam's mother was in town for Mother's Day and had decided to spend it with Alexie and her family. Janice made her way over to Christine, with Emma following behind, and introduced herself with the familiar rummaging bag Liam had created. Alexie went over to join them. The next two hours were spent with food, laughter, and stories, with glasses brimming over with Alexie's famous raspberry-rosemary lemonade.

Alexie noticed Emma in the yard by the garden boxes and headed out to check on her while her mom was being thoroughly entertained by her cousin Nicole and her aunt Janet.

"Hey... how's it going?" said Alexie to Emma.

"It's going okay. Why is that plant sitting off to the side?" asked Emma.

The plant had dried leaves and a few moldy spots on its stem. It didn't appear healthy, but it wasn't quite dead.

"I decided to move it. It was planted in a spot that didn't have the right type of soil and nutrients. It was also planted underneath a tree that blocked the sunlight it needed. It's going over there in the empty spot in the bed with the other plants that need bright sun most of the day. It won't take but a second. Help me do it really quick. It's a pepper plant that gives off a pretty hefty harvest," said Alexie.

"If you say so. It already looks dead to me. I don't think it's gonna make it," said Emma as she looked closer at the shriveled plant.

"It will make it. I see a little green in the stem. It just needs to be moved into the right atmosphere. Then we need to water it and keep the weeds back. It's been through a lot," said Alexie, picking up the plant gently with the digger.

She showed Emma how to gently peel off the dead leaves and loosen the roots. They planted it in the garden bed, sprinkled a little fertilizer around it, and Emma watered it.

As it still looked limp, Emma said, "I don't know. This one is a goner!"

"Give it some time. You'll see," said Alexie as they walked back to the house and rejoined the crowd.

Alexie felt a sigh of relief after everyone had left, and the day had been pleasant and uneventful. The house had been tidied by the last of the ladies who left. The only thing left to do was help Christine get to bed. The day was almost done. Christine was a little tuckered out from all the conversations and people. Alexie was brushing Christine's hair when Christine reached up and touched the scar on Alexie's eyebrow and then the tiny old scar on her face near her eye. Alexie recoiled.

"Such a pretty girl to have such scars. Did you fall off your bike as a youngin'?" asked Christine, not remembering she had caused all of them.

Alexie thought maybe now was a good time to bring back the old Christine and ask her what she'd been wanting to apologize for—what she knew involved her dad. Alexie breathed deeply as she fell back into the memory of her many facial scars, her eyes filling with tears she refused to let fall.

Alexie was eleven years old. She had merely entered the room where Christine was sitting in the dark, looking at a photo album filled with pictures of her father as she sobbed bitterly. Alexie came over and tried to comfort her mother.

"Don't cry, Ma. You said we'll see Dad again in heaven. You look at these every day and get so sad. Maybe we should just frame a few of your favorites..." Alexie grabbed her face as she recoiled and squealed in pain when Christine's ring gashed the corner of her eye socket as she hit her backhanded across the face.

"DON'T TELL ME WHAT TO DO, CHILD! YOU TALK TOO MUCH! If it weren't for you, he'd be HERE, and I wouldn't have to look in a book to see him! GET OUT!!! GET OUT OF MY SIGHT!" yelled Christine, not even noticing the blood running from Alexie's face.

Alexie ran to the kitchen and grabbed a piece of ice. She sat in her room for hours with her door closed, peering out her window, wishing she was somewhere else and someone else. She stayed home from school for the next two days, going into the weekend until the swelling went down, to keep questions at bay from the teachers. She needed a stitch or two, but they couldn't explain how it had happened without trouble, so she didn't get stitches or see a doctor.

Christine could barely look at Alexie for the next few days. She felt guilty, but not enough to apologize. Not enough to never let it happen again. The cut healed on its own without stitches, leaving a lifetime—though tiny—scar that required a lie whenever the "How did you get that?" question was asked. The inner scar in Alexie's soul was deeper. Bigger. Sharper.

"This scar came from you, Mom. Do you remember hitting me... and throwing books and dishes and things at me?" said Alexie, holding back the years of pain in her voice.

"What do you mean? Did your mother do that to you? That's awful," Christine asked, genuinely forgetting what she had done.

Alexie decided to leave it alone for today. Today was a good Mother's Day. Why wreck it all?

She decided not to stir the old Christine any further... at least not tonight.

"Yep, she did. Goodnight, Ma," she said while turning out the light and heading toward the door.

"Ya know I didn't mean it... I had a lot of troubles when you were little. I'm sorry," said Christine softly as she fluffed her pillow and turned toward the window, pulling the covers up to her neck.

Alexie stood still in the doorway. She decided to keep it a good night.

"I know, Ma. Good night, and Happy Mother's Day," said Alexie as she pulled the door closed.

Alexie went into the bathroom, washed her face, and stared at her small facial scars. She convinced herself it could have been much worse. But it also could have been so much better if her dad had not died. Today was a good day, she told herself. This memory was one of those seventy-seven times the Lord says to forgive, she thought. She forgave her mom again within her memory as she felt her anguish subside.

"Today was a good day," she said to herself out loud in the mirror five times. She pushed back her memories for the night, journaled in her "thankful" diary, and went to bed.

Chapter Twelve-
Before We Thrived...

L ater in the week, Liam and Emma came over for breakfast. Melinda was back and had Christine dressed and occupied on the back porch for the morning.

Liam went out to greet Christine and Melinda. Emma spotted the pepper plant they had replanted out back. She dashed out of the screened-in porch quickly with her ponytail trailing two seconds behind, with Alexie following after her.

"No way! It doesn't look sick anymore. It grew and now it looks healthy! It's starting to flower... like it's completely renewed! Is this the same plant? I was sure it was a goner!" said Emma as she gently touched the newly sprouted leaves.

"It just needed a new environment and a bit of care. Plants can be sensitive to their surroundings but also very resilient. Kinda like us," said Alexie, giving Emma a friendly shoulder nudge.

"Yeah. Like us... us?" Emma asked curiously, still not knowing much about Alexie's history.

"Yep... us. I'll tell you about it one day. But we both can thrive just like this pepper plant—in the right atmosphere, with safety, sun, and care... water, and a bit of pruning of things we don't need in our lives draining our energy... and don't forget fertilizer. Like this plant, we've gone through quite a bit of hardship... before we thrived... but it's not the end of our story. How are things at home with Liam?" asked Alexie.

"It's good. I don't feel stressed or scared. I'm safe with Dad. Do you think I could have my friend Sadie come down for a week in the summer?" Emma asked.

"I don't think your dad would mind that. Just ask him later. Grab a handful of mint for me before we go in, and do you mind throwing those peels and the old coffee grinds into the compost bin for me?"

"OK. What is compost used for? It smells horrible. I can't see anybody using rotting trash for anything!" Emma said with her nose scrunched.

"All that rotten trash will break down into nutrients and become fertilizer for the soil in our next garden batch. It's kind of a circle-of-life thing. What appears to be moldy trash eventually disintegrates into what the next crop needs to flourish. Even the healthiest plants sometimes need a little fertilizing to kick-start them to a new level... also kinda like us. Oh—and don't forget the ground-up eggshells I left in a bag on the counter... and don't forget the mint!" said Alexie.

Emma was learning the plants and garden well and walked toward the mint with scissors in hand. Liam and Alexie went to sit at the table with Christine and Melinda. Christine reached suddenly toward Alexie, only to grab her drinking cup. Alexie flinched and recoiled as if Christine were about to hit her—a common reflex she had developed as a child. Whenever Christine was nearby and her arms moved, Alexie would instinctively flinch, thinking she was about to be struck. Liam and Melinda stared intently at Alexie.

"I'll take Christine inside for a bit. It's getting hot outside anyway," said Melinda.

"Are you ok?" asked Liam. "I haven't seen you do that before."

"Do what? I'm fine. Just dealing with a lot of memories and such," said Alexie, grabbing a napkin to wipe crumbs from the table.

Liam sensed Alexie's discomfort and changed the subject. He had noticed the small facial scars she carried but had never asked how she got them. He figured she would eventually open up when she was ready. Today she still wasn't ready—but she was closer.

"Emma is getting settled in. She's been more talkative and less edgy lately. I wish I had gotten her earlier," said Liam.

"You didn't know. But she's doing so much better already. There's a lot to feeling safe with someone. She'll heal quicker in her new atmosphere, I hope."

"Yes, I hope she adjusts well to a new school."

"One month at a time! She'll enjoy the rest of the summer and make new friends, so the transition will be easier since she'll already have a couple of friends."

"True. But what about you? Do you feel safe with your mom being here, and is it healthy for you to care for her here? I don't think I realized how bad you had it as a kid with her. Are you going to be able to handle your mom... emotionally? It's your decision, and I'm willing to do whatever you feel we can handle. Just something to think about when you're ready."

"Why? You don't think I can handle it?"

"It's not that... you can. But because you can doesn't mean you should—especially at the risk of your own emotional and mental health. There are other options for her. You don't have to be the hero. We can still visit her frequently and make sure she's well taken care of somewhere nearby, and even bring her home for visits. I'm here for you whichever direction you choose," said Liam.

Alexie didn't answer as she played with the crumbs on the table. The conversation reminded her of the talk she'd recently had with Melinda, who understood the extent of the trauma she endured growing up with her mother. It echoed the conversations she had within herself on the bad days with Christine.

Those were the days she spent searching for respite care facilities online. The days she felt her joy diminish and her anxiety rise as old memories resurfaced. Alexie was determined to at least try and give it her best. Christine was her mother, and she owed it to her to try. How much more "try" she had left in her—that was the real question.

Chapter Thirteen-
Walks, Wine &
Emotional Affairs

Alexie had waited long enough to catch up with Deidre. She pulled into the parking lot and climbed the slight hill. While she waited, Alexie admired the chain-linked fence wall filled with locks and lockets representing eternal love. Some had signatures, others didn't—big and small locks of different shapes, sizes, and colors. She thought it would make a perfect date walk for her and Liam, a place to pledge their love with a unique lock that no one could remove.

Deidre climbed the hill wearing her sunhat and shades. She jogged the last few steps to catch up with Alexie as they began crossing over Lake Murray Dam together.

Deidre plugged her finger in her right ear. "This traffic should die down soon since lunch is almost over. How are things with Liam... and your mom... and gosh, Emma? I feel like we have so much to catch up on!" she said, tugging her sunhat down to keep the wind from snatching it away.

"Oh no, I have tons to tell you, but you first! I want to know how you and Bryan are doing. Y'all looked fine at dinner, but you had that little crinkle over your left brow that told me otherwise," Alexie said.

"Well, you know me too well. I don't even know where to start. We've been together so long, and I can't imagine myself with anybody else. I want us to make it work. But I don't know if we will. He is so naïve when it comes to protecting our relationship."

"Deidre, what do you mean? Bryan hasn't cheated, right? He doesn't strike me as the type. He seems to value marriage," Alexie said, grabbing her baseball cap as the wind lifted it. "At least when we're together, y'all seem so happy."

"We *are* happy—until he comes home talking about the woman at work he had lunch with and everything they discussed. And then a couple times a day, I catch him texting her with this excited smirk on his face, telling her every little thing. I would never have lunch alone with another guy like it was nothing. That's where trouble starts. First lunch, then dinner, and before you know it, you've got a new best friend you're accidentally falling in love with. Then people ask, 'How did this happen?' Well, it started when you first agreed to lunch. Then dinner. And God forbid—drinks!

"He even brought home a food container that wasn't mine. She made some ooey-gooey dessert she wanted him to try. Can you believe he sees nothing wrong with it? It was an ooey-gooey, chocolatey, caramel, decadent dessert! He doesn't see she's trying to reel him in. And he had the nerve to leave a few bites for me to try! Clueless."

"So... have y'all been arguing about it? Like before? You know—when he was walking the neighborhood with your gorgeous neighbor and the dogs?" Alexie asked.

"Yep. He insists she's just a friend and that I'm being insecure. This chick knows my birthday and all kinds of personal things I didn't expect him to tell anyone—let alone *her*. He accuses me of being controlling because I want him to cut her off completely. But I guess he values her friendship too much to do that. Can you get Liam to talk to him again? Bryan actually listened to him last time about that other chick and finally realized it wasn't good for us. Nothing happened, but I *know* something would have if he'd kept on.

"This time is worse. I constantly catch him texting her, and he thinks it's okay because he isn't hiding it. He's too excited to talk to her. I'm close to giving her some kind of wifey warning! And I don't believe in that whole work-wife mess. Folks laugh about it, but it ain't cute, and it's dangerous."

"Yeah, it *is* dangerous—and desensitizing. I'll ask Liam to talk to him, but they've probably already discussed it. It always helps to ask, 'What if the shoe was on the other foot?'" Alexie said.

"But how do I say it so it sticks this time? He shouldn't have to be told to be considerate and to protect our relationship," Deidre said, her face puzzled.

"Well... you could ask how he'd feel if *you* were having lunch with some guy at work, and he was bringing you food, and you were discussing your home life over dinner and drinks. Ask him how he would feel—and what that guy's intentions might be. Sometimes men are a little naïve. So ask him how *he* would feel if you had that kind of friendship with a coworker. Sometimes guys go too far trying to be nice—and fall right into the work-wife trap. It might wake him up to the danger of emotional affairs," Alexie said.

"An emotional affair. I didn't think of it that way. It *is* an affair. Yeah... we're going to have to get help with this one," Deidre said as her pace slowed, sadness softening her face as her eyes filled with tears.

"I'm sorry to be so blunt. Maybe I'm wrong, but you guys should get counseling before it gets out of hand—even aside from him talking to Liam. Protecting your emotional bond is important. We talked to Pastor Ellis and his wife, and it helped us a lot. Guys can be just as cunning when they're trying to slide their way into our lives. And sometimes it's accidental, not intentional. You can develop feelings for people when you spend too much one-on-one time with them. Maybe they don't *start* falling for you, but it can end up that way. It always leads to something.

"It's all about keeping healthy boundaries for the sake of your relationship—and protecting your spiritual side too. It's hard stepping away from what the world calls normal. Y'all should make an appointment. And maybe see if he wants to connect with some guys once a month for a men's Bible study or hang out with someone with a spiritual mindset. Counseling never hurt anyone. It can only help," Alexie said.

Alexie grew quiet for a moment, hearing her own words echo Liam's. He always nudged her toward therapy to help her process her upbringing. She knew that if anything ever threatened her relationship with Liam, she would get therapy—but she thought she was processing things just fine. She pushed the thought aside, convincing herself her situation was different and under control.

"Yeah, I guess. None of that can hurt. We'll see what he says. We gotta move back this way. We need a strong atmosphere. I could use a glass of wine!" Deidre said.

"Save it for the wine tasting we'll do in Greenville. Y'all need to get things straightened out by then so you can enjoy the day, forgive, and move on. Sorry to sound selfish. But you know—don't let the sun go down while you're still angry. You never know the last time you may see someone... like what happened with my dad. I wish y'all could move back this way soon too," Alexie said.

"I'm praying we do. Most of our family is here. And we both could use a change of scenery. Bryan needs somebody close by to talk some sense into him. So... what's going on with you guys?" Deidre asked.

Alexie caught Deidre up on the ups and downs with her mom, the debate about placing her in a facility, and Emma's plan to move in with them after the wedding.

"Wow. That's a lot to handle in a new marriage. You'll need plenty of girls' day outs for stress relief. So how are you and Emma doing together?" Deidre asked.

"We're connecting well. We have a lot in common. I just want her to be okay, you know? Whatever it takes. She can't stay with her mom another day—not after what we found out. She's blessed to be doing as well as she is. And she loves it here."

"That's great. But expect a few surprises as you get to know her better. Kids don't go through all that without developing some coping issues."

"What do you mean? I think she's coping fine... especially considering everything."

"Well, think about it. Do you really think she's being honest about none of those men getting to her? Especially when she was younger? She may have blocked some of those memories," Deidre said.

"If she has, it'll come out in due time—when she's ready. And maybe when she feels safe enough to talk about them. Or maybe she won't talk about them at all. Maybe she'll want to put it behind her and start fresh. After everything Liam has done for me while dealing with my mom... whatever comes with her in the future, I'll just be there for her. That's what she needs. A safe space. A place where she can be a kid without fear or misery. I wish I had..."

Alexie stopped mid-sentence, staring out at the lake while gripping her hat to keep the wind from taking it.

"Well, that was a good walk. We need to walk the park next time you're back. And maybe look at a few neighborhoods for houses. Hey, don't fret too much about Bryan. He's just naïve. If there was something real to hide, you probably wouldn't know about her. It'll work out. I'm going to manifest in faithful prayer that y'all move back here soon!" Alexie said.

"You wished you had what?" Deidre asked, not letting her get away with avoidance.

"Somebody to look out for me when I needed it, that's all. Someone who could see I needed to be rescued. Okay... enough deep talk for today. What are you wearing to Greenville?" Alexie said.

They hugged and said their goodbyes, awaiting the upcoming Trip Day.

Chapter Fourteen- The Drive By and the Day Trip

A lexie drove home to find Melinda and Christine walking down the street. She waved, and Melinda returned the gesture warmly. Inside, Alexie headed to the back porch and settled into the chair in the corner. She admired her handmade butterfly—or dragonfly, or firefly—art hanging on the wall. Some days it was one or the others depending on the angle and mood of the day.

Alexie sat and enjoyed her yard for a while, mulling over landscape designs she was working on for a few neighbors. Life wasn't so bad when Christine and Melinda were out walking. She pondered what things would be like soon with a full-grown teen and an aging mother under the same roof. She savored the quiet moments when the house was hers alone.

She pulled out her wedding idea books—something she rarely had time for anymore with her new pace of life. She gave herself a good half hour to daydream about her long-awaited day.

Eventually, she went to tidy the front porch. Squinting toward the end of the block, she froze. *Was that a for-sale sign?* How had she missed that when she drove in? Sure enough, it was. She'd have to visit the Coopers soon to see where they were headed.

She couldn't help wondering whether that house might be perfect for Deidre and Bryan. The thought made her chuckle—imagining speaking or praying it into existence. How wonderful it would be to have them as neighbors. She couldn't wait to tell Deidre.

She picked up her gray watering can from the blue tray—*Dad's tray,* she thought—and gently set the memories aside. She'd been learning to do that more often when she needed to enjoy the present moment. She figured she only had a few minutes before Melinda returned with Christine. She watered the porch plants, then stepped into the yard to pluck a few blueberries from her bushes. She sat on the swing and ate them by hand.

Her phone buzzed with a text from Melinda.

"I'm going to take Christine with me to do a little grocery shopping before I go home. That way I can relax when I get home and not go back out. I hope you don't mind."

Alexie let out a big sigh. *What would I do without Melinda and her thoughtfulness?* She stayed on the swing for another hour before they returned, admiring her rosemary and blueberry bushes and the landscape design she'd created. The hummingbirds and other wildlife were unusually active. She even heard a familiar hoot from Hoot, her resident owl.

Maybe today he'll finally show himself. She longed to see the owl whose call she heard so often. He had managed to stay hidden for so long.

Alexie went back into the kitchen and made another batch of her famous raspberry–rosemary punch. She grabbed a devotional book and a blanket, then settled on the floor in front of the couch.

Today was one of the better days. After reading her devotional, she decided to sit on the front porch again and watch the hummingbirds.

But as she eased onto the bench with her book and a half cup of blueberries, she noticed two cars driving slowly toward the house.

The second car was familiar.

Alexie's heart plummeted as she tried to steady her breathing.

It was Kevin.

He drove past slowly, turning his head toward her with that same arrogant familiar smirk. The other car was the woman from the restaurant.

Alexie stepped off the porch as both cars continued down the street and turned into the driveway of the house with the for-sale sign. The woman got out with a clipboard and unlocked the realtor box. *Was she showing Kevin the house?* She went inside first, and Kevin looked up the block at Alexie and waved.

Alexie's heart raced. She ran into the house and called Liam.

"I don't understand why he would want to be on the same street! I can't... He is determined to stalk me forever. I thought he was moving on... I don't feel safe..."

"Hey, it's okay," Liam said. "I guess he didn't get the message last time. His narcissism won't let me have the last word. He will never hurt you as long as I'm alive—I promise. Lock all the doors until Melinda gets back. I'm going to handle this."

"Handle it how? I don't want you getting into a fight with him or getting hurt. We'll just have to deal with it. I'll get extra cameras... and maybe we should get a dog," Alexie said, wiping away tears.

"I'll be over shortly. Call me—or 911—if you notice anything else."

Alexie pulled the blinds and peeked outside as both cars drove back up the street, a little faster this time. She sat on the living room floor practicing deep breathing to calm herself. There was nothing she could do. She silently prayed he wouldn't get the house and that any deal would fall through.

A few days passed with no sign of Kevin returning. She decided to put it behind her and focus on enjoying her long-awaited Greenville trip. Still, she tossed and turned at night, unable to sleep. Maybe Liam was right that Kevin needed to have the last word and would eventually leave her alone.

She decided to cut off all thoughts that fed worry or anxiety about him. Letting those thoughts linger felt like giving him a kind of power—power she refused to let him have. Tomorrow, she told herself, she'd journal, pray, and distract herself with planning her new business whenever he crossed her mind.

She prayed and breathed deeply until sleep finally came.

Liam called and woke her the next morning; Alexie had purposely slept in so she could feel rested and renewed.

"I just want you to know that you don't have to worry about Kevin moving in down the street. I tracked down the real estate lady he's been hanging around with," said Liam.

"Really? How do you know?" Alexie perked up, sitting upright in bed with her hair completely disheveled.

"Well, I found her number and called her. I asked a lot of questions about the house—pretending I was interested—just to see if Kevin was looking at it. Actually, I'd talked with Bryan, and he saw the sign too. He asked about it like it might be an option for him and Deidre. I mentioned I'd heard someone was planning to make an offer, and the agent said she didn't know who that could be. She said she and her new assistant had viewed the house recently, but she wasn't aware of any offers." Liam paused. "Apparently, Kevin is training with her to see if he wants to dabble in real estate. So I don't think he's trying to buy the house. He probably just used the showing as an excuse to mess with you—or with us."

"Thank God. I've got to stop letting him get to me like that. I really thought I was doing better, but the idea of him living nearby sent me into a tailspin. Thank God—and thank you for looking into it. I hope somebody buys that house soon so we don't have to keep wondering what he'll do next," said Alexie.

"I don't think you have to worry," said Liam reassuringly. "I highly doubt he wants to look me in the eyes every day—not after our last conversation. I think he still gets high off subtle harassment. I made sure she knew my name, so if she mentions me to him, he'll know I see him. So let's put it behind us for now."

Alexie sat up in bed hugging her pillow. They talked about the food tour they'd chosen for Greenville and all the little shops they wanted to stop by. It would be the perfect time to take photos at the park by the waterfall. Christine was taken care of for the day, and Emma would spend time next door. They'd be home just before sunset. After saying their goodbyes, Alexie started getting ready.

Deidre and Bryan had arrived back in town for the trip. They drove two cars for their quadruple date: Deidre, Alexie, Bryan, and Liam in one; Carla, Renee, Tyler, and Chase from church in the other. Nicole volunteered to watch Christine so all their friends could join them. Alexie loved Greenville. It was only an hour and fifteen minutes away but felt like another state entirely—a place with its own pulse, rhythm, and buzzing nightlife. She needed this day trip. Finally, the day had arrived.

Alexie needed Deidre and Bryan to be in a better place—and they were, or at least they acted like it. They listened to their favorite playlist, sang along, and reminisced about their college days. The trip passed quickly. They parked and found a large table in the Square in front of the ice cream shop. Alexie loved the smell of caramel and freshly made chocolate turtles drifting through the air.

She tried to remind herself not to eat too many of those turtles—her wedding dress might get snug—but then thought, what the heck. She'd pushed the wedding date back, and with all the walking they'd be doing, she would burn it off. Chocolate-drizzled pretzels and all her favorite ice cream flavors were under one roof.

They all sampled small bites of whatever they wanted. Alexie loved that Liam never fixated on her weight or her so-called imperfections. She never had to tiptoe around unrealistic expectations like she did with Kevin. Liam loved her—two extra pounds and all. He encouraged her to fully enjoy the food experience—not in a gluttonous way, but as a simple celebration of what was ahead.

Eventually, they wandered down the street toward the scent of New York-style pizza. They agreed to grab some on their way home. They didn't want to get too full before the official food tour began. Their first stop was a quaint restaurant tucked down a side street, complete with a brief history of the building and the creamiest shrimp and grits.

Alexie and Liam leaned in, whispering about the quick connection forming between Carla and Chase. The two were so wrapped up in conversation and laughter that they didn't notice they were being observed.

They finally reached their last stop, where they enjoyed a customized drink and a beautifully cooked piece of pork belly inside a hidden speakeasy. During dinner, Liam's phone chimed. Alexie noticed the way he read his messages with quiet discretion; his expression edged with unease. She tucked the thought away and decided to enjoy the day.

She admired the carefully planned foliage lining the clean streets and took pictures, hoping to recreate some of the designs in her own backyard. It was one of the reasons Greenville remained one of her favorite places.

They walked back uphill on Main Street until they reached the free concert at the hotel square where they'd sat earlier and found an empty table. Curiosity eventually got the best of her—tucking the thought away wasn't working when it came to Liam.

"Hey, who was that texting earlier? You got quite a few messages," Alexie asked, unable to hide the curiosity in her voice.

"Oh—it was my cousin. You know my aunt didn't have kids, so he's excited about the inheritance she divided up. Turns out I have a small one I didn't know about too. I just didn't want to bring it up in front of everyone, and honestly... who wants to talk about an inheritance on a getaway trip? I'll fill you in once I know more," whispered Liam.

"Oh wow. Okay... we can talk later," said Alexie, tapping her foot to the old-school live music.

It felt like the perfect day. Later, they would walk back downhill to the park to take photos on the bridge by the waterfall. Deidre and Bryan still appeared to be in a good place—at least from what Alexie could see. Maybe they had worked things out, or maybe, like before, they were simply putting it aside so the trip wouldn't be ruined. Alexie hoped they truly had resolved their boundaries.

Watching them look happy reminded Alexie that soon she would be bound to Liam. She would be Mrs. Liam Bradsworth. She often felt favored by God to have found him, especially after surviving Kevin and a difficult childhood. She knew she could not let her past interfere with what she had now. What was the point of surviving a painful childhood and an emotionally abusive relationship if her mind still lived in bondage to both?

She was determined to have the full life she'd been promised—after blood, sweat, tears, and even death; as she told Emma they would thrive.

Alexie's phone chimed.

"Hey cuz! Everything okay?" she asked hopefully.

"Hey... well... what time did you say y'all were coming back? Aunt Christine is a handful today. I can barely get her to sit down. I usually only sit with her for a couple hours. She's agitated. She pushed me. She keeps insisting she's looking for her baby—I guess she's reverted to when you were an infant. I'm sorry, I didn't want to call, but I don't know how much more of this I can take. It's been four hours and I'm worried she might slip out the front door while I'm in the bathroom. How do you do this every day?" said Nicole.

"Take her out on the back porch. I have several stations to keep her busy and safe. But please keep an eye on her so she doesn't try to leave the house. We're leaving in a few minutes and can be home just over an hour after that. Call me if it gets worse. And thanks for hanging in there," said Alexie with a hint of anxiety.

"Hey guys," Alexie said, turning to the group. "I hate to cut the trip short... but Mom is sundowning really badly, and I don't know how much longer my cousin can handle her. Do you mind if we head back earlier than planned? I'm so sorry, y'all. Looks like we won't have time to stop at Barnes and Noble. I'll have to restock my journals next trip."

Everyone understood but was disappointed about missing the bookstore. Alexie loved the thought of lounging in the café or sitting on the floor while browsing for a good book for her newly cleaned-out shelf. It would have to wait. They grabbed a pizza to go for the road and headed back toward Lake Murray.

Alexie tried to stay upbeat, joining in the conversation, but her thoughts kept drifting back to caring for her mother. Her journaling and Bible studies had taught her to remember the good: at least they enjoyed most of the trip. They could always come back when she had more experienced help with Christine. It was still a great day—just cut short. She wished Nicole had taken the local class she'd recommended last month on caring for people with dementia.

When they arrived, the front door was cracked open. Alexie stepped inside, and Nicole met her in the hallway with her purse over her shoulder, ready to leave.

"She's in the living room. I don't know how you do this day in and day out. She asked me the same questions at least eighty times, and I had to redirect her from going out the front door several times. I've locked it four times! I didn't think evenings would be this hard... I'm sorry, Lex, but I just can't," said Nicole, exhausted.

"It's okay. Maybe I should've told you more of what to expect. I was hoping I could get away for a day without incident. This is why I'm going to have to do something," Alexie said, flopping onto the couch. "Where is she now?"

"Well, she's wandered into another part of the house. I'm exhausted, Lex. I gotta go. I hope y'all had fun. Let's catch up later.

I want to help, but I had no idea. And yeah—I should've taken that class you mentioned," said Nicole.

Alexie wanted to say thank you, but she battled what she really felt and decided silence was safer. She felt Nicole could have managed two more hours, especially after they'd looked forward to this trip for months. She hated imagining a life where she could never leave the house for more than a few hours. The constant vigilance was draining. She needed to find a way to live her life while caring for Christine. She also knew she probably *should* have warned Nicole how difficult the evenings could be—but if she had, Nicole might have backed out.

She called Liam to vent, but he didn't answer. That was unusual. First the secretive texting, now ignoring her call. A familiar fear crept in—maybe Liam was pulling back. Maybe the reality of the "package deal" that came with their marriage was becoming too much.

The next day, Liam called.

"Hey, how was your mom when you got in last night?" he asked.

"She was pretty agitated. Nicole bolted out the door the second I walked in. I guess she won't volunteer again anytime soon. I called you last night to talk about it," Alexie said.

"Oh—I think I was on the phone and missed your call. I'm still getting late-night calls about my family's property. It's surprising, honestly. I texted you last night to check in. I know we're trying to avoid long late-night calls—it helps us keep our purity straight until the wedding. But maybe I should've called back just for a minute to make sure you were okay. I've been distracted lately. Are you okay?" said Liam.

"I'm better. Just a little down. Yesterday was fun until that call. I got pictures of some plants I didn't recognize—maybe Tess can help me figure them out. And I think I found a drink combination for the wedding! Hey, let's catch up later. Mom's still a bit off from last night, and Melinda's coming over, so I need to fill her in," said Alexie.

Chapter Fifteen-
Melinda's Maybe
Secret

Melinda came in with several bags full of snacks and activities for Christine, placing them onto the kitchen island. She unpacked a few items while chatting about how beautiful the weather was outside, glancing over at Alexie sitting at the kitchen table with a cup of rosemary green tea.

"Hey, Alexie...you okay today? I think Christine is still asleep. Must've been a doozy of a day for her," she said, watching Alexie stir her tea with a hint of sadness.

"I'm alright, I guess. You know...I want to do my best to care for Mom, and I want a normal, happy life with Liam. This doesn't feel normal. I just hope I can have both without feeling like I need to sacrifice one," said Alexie.

"I don't think Mr. Liam would ever ask you to sacrifice your mom. He's too good for that. I think you may just need to explore a creative plan to care for your mom and still enjoy being a newlywed. And define normal. Normal's different for everybody," Melinda said warmly.

"I don't know if I can. Maybe I don't even know what normal looks like," said Alexie.

"I think aging and illness are a stage of life that affects everyone around the person going through it, but I've seen many people learn to navigate it—almost master it—minus a few bad days here and there. And I'm gonna need y'all to reschedule that Greenville trip on a day when *I* can be with Mrs. Christine all day! What were you thinking asking Nicole?" Melinda said, giving Alexie a side-eye and a smirk as she joined her at the table.

"She wanted to help, and I should've known better. I appreciate it and will take you up on the offer—with extra pay, of course. There's just so much going on. Liam's starting to be occupied by family issues too. And I'll probably never find out what Mom has been trying to apologize to me about regarding my dad. It's been driving me crazy, but whenever I get close, the dementia takes over. I guess it was never meant for me to know," she said, pushing her bangs out of her face before sipping her tea.

"You mean the thing about your father's death?" Melinda asked hesitantly.

"Yeah...how do you know? Did she say something?" Alexie said, sitting up straighter, anticipation sharpening her posture.

"Well, actually...I think she did. I didn't want to say nothin', because the mind gets so scrambled with dementia. I didn't know how much weight it carried. But I spend a lot of time with her, and there were many times she talked to me as if I were you. She apologized for something pretty big. But it may or may not—"

"Melinda! Whether it's true or not, you have to tell me. Let *me* decide if she's confused. This has driven me crazy for too long," Alexie said anxiously. "What was she apologizing for?"

"Okay, but remember—this could've been the dementia talking. She thought I was you, and she said she was sorry for having so many issues when you were young. She said she couldn't handle taking responsibility for your father's death. Your dad didn't die in the car accident on the way to pick you up from school. She said he died on the way back from the grocery store after a brief argument, where she insisted he go that day. She said her life hasn't been the same since. Now remember—we don't know if she was lucid or confused," Melinda explained.

Alexie covered her mouth with both hands and sobbed deeply.

"What?...all those years she blamed me and treated me horribly," she cried.

Christine walked into the kitchen and sat at the table. "Why is such a pretty girl like you crying?"

She reached for a napkin to dab Alexie's tears, but Alexie pulled away and stood.

"I can't...I can't take care of her right now after knowing this. How could she..." Alexie said as she walked out of the kitchen, still sobbing, heading toward her bedroom. The hallway felt longer with every step. She reached her bed and cried until she fell asleep.

When she woke up, she found a note on her nightstand from Melinda apologizing and saying she hoped she hadn't caused too much pain. She also mentioned she'd be out with Christine most of the day to give her space to process.

Alexie felt the temptation to stay in bed for a long while, maybe longer than she should. She pushed herself to get up, put on her walking shoes, and drove to the park. She sat staring at the bright yellow mini house for too long. Finally, she got out and walked the path, arms crossed as she remembered her father and wished he were still there. Memories of her mother's overt and subtle abuse surfaced. She circled the yellow house twice, beginning to process the unnecessary guilt she'd carried for years.

She wasn't ready to go home. Instead, she drove toward Lake Murray and parked on the farthest side of the lake. She didn't even remember the drive. Facing the water, she grabbed her wide-brimmed hat and took in the long row of love locks fastened to the gate, swaying slightly above the gentle waves of the day. She had seen them many times before. Thoughts of Liam crossed her mind.

She continued walking toward the other side, lowering her head whenever someone passed, hoping they wouldn't notice the grief etched into her eyes.

She finally made it across—less angry now, but more hurt. She climbed onto the picnic table, gazing at the rocks supporting the lake's boundaries. She sat with herself and with the leftover anger and hurt. She thought, cried, and prayed her way through a few feelings. It was somewhat freeing to know she was not the cause of her father's death but crushing to face the extent of her mother's cruelty.

Secretly, she wished her mother was confused. She wasn't sure which was worse. She knew she would need many more walk days and a couple of new writing journals to process her way back to normal functioning. But she would get there, as she always did. She would eventually tell Liam, but first she needed to process this on her own and with God—without anyone's influence. She would talk to Liam and her friends when she was ready.

Alexie wiped the sweat from her brow as she walked back into the kitchen, hanging her walking and gardening hat on the hook on her mudroom wall. Melinda was sitting at the kitchen table with a cup of tea and another empty cup waiting for Alexie to return.

"I hope you won't mind, but I asked Liam for funds to send your mom to a respite day spot where I used to take my husband on a really bad day," said Melinda cautiously as she poured a cup of chamomile tea for Alexie. "They took good care of him for eight hours. I felt you needed it. I didn't tell Liam why—just that Christine was having another off day and we could use a short break. She'll be back this evenin', and I thought we could talk a bit."

"Thanks," Alexie said in an exhausted whisper, pulling off her walking shoes.

"You know, if this is true, I don't know what to say other than sometimes folks just don't do right," Melinda continued. "They may know better—or maybe not. They may be so traumatized or damaged in their heart that they feel the need to lash out and make others miserable along with 'em. I'm not making excuses, just trying to make sense of it along with ya. But I do know she loved you enough to try to apologize in the midst of dementia, whether it was true or just in her head. I hope you can find a way to let it go. Don't you think this has taken enough time and attention in your life and heart? People do ugly and horrible things. We live in a fallen world. We can let it ruin our life and peace, or we can accept other people's messiness for what it is. You know in all things God has a way of working things out... let me hush... I'm always preachin' too much."

"But what would cause her to do such a thing?" Alexie asked. "Hatred? Some kind of weird jealousy of your own daughter? But I know you're right, Melinda. Does the 'why' really make a difference? It doesn't change what I went through. If I weren't a Christian, I probably wouldn't have returned the call I got that day to check on my mom. I probably would never speak to her again, let alone be concerned about her care or her dementia. But I am... so I do. But I refuse to let this take any more of my life. I'm going to figure out how to move on. Just not tonight. I'm too exhausted. Thank you for everything you've done. I couldn't get through this without you." She reached across the table and patted Melinda's soft, wrinkled hands.

Melinda picked up Christine from the daily respite care facility and helped her shower and get into bed before leaving for the night.

Alexie stood propped in the doorway, watching her mom, who was nearly asleep. She stepped into the room and sat on the edge of her mother's bed. Christine was drowsy but still awake.

"Mom, I don't know if I can forgive you tonight. I know I should, but I am determined that I will eventually," Alexie said, not caring whether she was speaking to the old Christine or the new pleasant one. "But I need to get this out. How could you make me carry guilt like that all those years? What did I do to deserve... never mind. I know there is nothing I did to deserve that kind of treatment. Mom, we are going to start over... soon... I am going to let this go. It's been a long day."

Alexie reached over her mother's head to turn out the light. This was the first time she couldn't tell which Christine she was talking to. Her mother stared blankly at the ceiling fan—no expression, no words. Maybe it was better that she didn't know which Christine was present.

Chapter Sixteen- Black Smoke

Alexie fell asleep after an emotionally exhausting day. She drifted off into her dreams again. Tonight, she dreamed the same dream of chasing her father in his familiar plaid shirt, hearing herself crying—but this time she almost caught him. He stopped, turned, and waited for her. She jumped into his arms as a little girl, the way he used to hold her on his hip when they grilled burgers together. She awakened to the smell of smoke.

Alexie lay still for a moment, trying to figure out if she was smelling grill smoke from her father's shirt in the dream, when she realized she smelled real smoke coming from the hallway. She opened the door, and black smoke rolled into her bedroom. Alexie ran, crouched and coughing, into the hallway, calling out for her mother.

She quickly saw the smoke coming from the kitchen and realized it wasn't as bad as she feared. A frying pan sat on the stove, smoldering with singed eggs, and a kitchen towel touching the pan had ignited on the highest heat. Alexie grabbed the fire extinguisher from under the cabinet, knocking its contents onto the floor. She sprayed the pan, moved it off the burner, and dropped it into the kitchen sink, feeling the heat through the handle.

"What's all that noise? I was making eggs for your dad," said Christine, sitting in the living room chair. "Did they burn?" she added, coughing and waving smoke from her face, still unalarmed. Alexie leaned against the kitchen sink, both hands covering her face.

"You know your dad always liked you better... I had to beg him to go to the store for me, but if you asked him to pick you up early from school, he never flinched," said the old Christine sternly from the couch. "He took the time to carve you a handmade tea tray, and all I ever got was quick-pick jewelry that I had no place to wear. But I'm still gonna make him his dang eggs before he goes to work this morning," she said, turning her head away from Alexie in disdain.

"Mom, it's three A.M.! Let's go back to bed. Um... Dad's not up yet for work," Alexie said, opening a window and avoiding triggering grief by reminding Christine he had passed.

"He's already up. I saw him walking down the hallway near your room a while ago. He said good morning to you before he even acknowledged me," Christine insisted.

Alexie froze as she remembered her dream. "Maybe you were dreaming too, Mom."

She was able to coax Christine back to bed, only then realizing she had forgotten to set her mother's bed alarm after the emotional events of the day. Alexie decided to set an alarm on her phone to remind herself to activate the bed alarm each night. She now had to set an alarm to set the other alarms. She could no longer afford to forget.

Alexie lay restless in bed. She reached up to turn on her lamp, opened her bedside drawer, then leaned over to crack her window to clear the smoke lingering in her room. She thought of her most recent conversations with Melinda. She picked up her Bible and her journal. She read, prayed, processed, and wrote. She did several deep-breathing exercises before returning to the kitchen for her sleepy tea.

She glanced at her intricately carved blue tray before returning to her room. Then she slept.

Chapter Seventeen-
Just Processing

F our complete prayer journals, many talks and long walks with girlfriends, and an entire garden harvest later.

Chapter Eighteen-
Suspicion and Leftover
Trauma

Alexie carried her blue tray with tea and her homemade chicken salad sandwiches to the back porch. Melinda nodded in approval as she and Christine sat far back in the swing, tying bundles of rosemary to dry. Alexie was waiting for Liam to come over for lunch and conversation. She gently shooed away a wasp attempting to enter the porch. She had watered her plants and made her usual batch of raspberry rosemary lemonade—a usual sign of her hospitality mood. She had several landscape appointments later in the week and looked forward to them, marveling at her new steady income.

Liam entered through the back door with Emma. Alexie and Emma took a quick garden tour to show her the ripened vegetables and herbs. Emma squinted toward the backyard and noticed six new fruit trees: peach and apple varieties, a blackberry bush, and a fig tree. She could hardly believe the peach trees already bore fruit. Alexie realized she was training her new assistant. Emma had been naturally drawn to the garden from the beginning and loved learning; it was also therapeutic for her. Emma joined Melinda and

Christine out back, harvesting herbs and fruits, while Liam and Alexie sat on the porch bench.

"Hey, she started growing things in pots at my place. She's definitely your new intern for the summer, and she's loving it!" said Liam enthusiastically. "She seems much more relaxed and happier here. I can't wait to get this court thing done. Speaking of being more relaxed—how are you feeling? You seem at peace."

"I'm getting there. I need to get a few things out of the way to be completely present. I have a few things I want to share with you. I know you've been considerate and patient with me—everyone else I know would have asked. I understand why you didn't. I want to tell you how I got these facial scars, starting with the obvious one on my eyebrow," said Alexie.

Liam listened silently, careful not to trigger anything she wasn't ready to share. Listening and anticipating her needs was his relational strength. He heard how a book thrown at her face had injured her eyebrow, leaving a permanent scar, along with the details of her eye scar and two other small facial marks. He absorbed her story with patient, silent respect. Alexie's eyes welled with tears, a relief from hiding them as if they were her fault.

After listening, Liam shared the hurts from his previous divorce from Lisa, which had scarred him emotionally and created insecurities as a father and future husband—unseen scars that surfaced in triggered behaviors. They listened to each other and vowed never to hide painful experiences again.

They felt an intimacy they had never experienced before. Grateful that friends and relatives were occupied in the yard, they scooted slightly apart on the porch bench. They had maintained purity in their relationship, but as their wedding date approached, it became more challenging, especially as they grew closer in spirit.

They guarded their time together at home by keeping others nearby, valuing the depth of their relationship, built on trust and godly commitment, and did not want to endanger their vows.

Melinda appeared increasingly committed to Christine, even showing up on her days off to visit or bring her famous bread pudding. Caring for others was her true calling, and she had mastered it through life experience. She was a blessing in disguise for Alexie, who could now slowly build her new business while tending to Christine's growing dementia needs with Melinda's devoted help. Melinda was her greatest source of respite.

Alexie felt she had learned enough from her gardening experience to teach classes on seed planting, garden variety, and care. Her services were in high demand due to people's desire for healthy, pesticide-free food and the struggling economy. Everyone with even an inch of dirt in their yard wanted a garden to offset grocery costs. Some wanted to learn to plant, while others desired the luxury of coming home to a fully planted garden by Alexie, leaving them only to water and weed.

She brainstormed the raised garden bed market. She planted a raised bed box full of specific flowers she wanted to cut and use at the wedding. She would also cut from her many shades of blue hydrangea bushes. She thought of selling cut flower bunches at the local market—all of it keeping Alexie pleasantly distracted from any leftover trauma. For now.

Alexie and Liam had a craving for the smoked chicken at the barbecue spot in Prosperity, so they rode out and enjoyed a quick lunch. On the way back toward Ballentine, they visited the local nurseries to squeeze in just a few more fruit trees. While looking at plum and pear varieties outside, Liam got a phone call and quickly stepped away from Alexie. She watched him intently as he walked farther away, while she tried to move closer to hear his whispering conversation. She was almost sure she heard a woman's voice. She decided she was overreacting—but as usual, she just had to ask.

"Who was that?" she asked in a very matter-of-fact tone.

"Just someone from work. I'm working on a project, and I just needed to focus for a few minutes. You know, maybe we have enough fruit trees. We wouldn't want to crowd the property and create too much extra work," said Liam hesitantly.

"Since when did you feel the yard was too much work? You've been encouraging me to expand the garden for half the year," she said, curious with a hint of anger.

"I was just thinking we shouldn't overdo it for resale purposes. For a gardener, the property is a dream yard. But for someone who doesn't want to work the yard too hard, it's a deterrent. Don't you think it would be best to keep it somewhat modest?"

"Modest? The property? You used to call it our house. Now it's the property... and why all this talk about resale? Is there something we need to discuss? Are we okay?" she said, stepping closer to Liam to read his body language.

"Oh no. It's nothing like that. I was just thinking about our home value and such," he said, looking away.

Alexie had mastered tucking things away for a bit when she needed to. She decided this was a conversation for another time; she didn't want to be distracted from the yard plan and continued looking for the proper trees. She came across a Meyer lemon tree and searched for a large pot for it. She remembered a neighbor who had grown one successfully by covering it in the winter to keep the frost at bay.

The Carolinas did not have the proper temperatures for citrus growth, but she had tasted her neighbor's home-grown lemons. She was determined to make it happen. She couldn't shake the thought of having her own fresh lemon supply. Liam rustled the change in his pocket as she continued to carefully inspect the fruit trees.

On the ride home, Alexie peeked through the sunrays out of the car window, deep in thought over Liam's behavior. She wondered if the thought of her past and living with her mother was beginning to give Liam second thoughts about their future. She tried hard not to be overtaken by doubt and suspicion.

She pretended to be unbothered for the remainder of the ride. As he dropped her off, his phone rang again. Liam gave her a quick goodbye and said he would call her later because he needed to catch the call. He drove away whispering again. What could this mean for Alexie and Liam?

Alexie called Deidre as soon as she kicked off her sandals.

"Hey, I need to talk. Something is going on with Liam. He's been taking several phone calls and walking away when the phone rings. And I'm sure it was a woman's voice. It's making me anxious. Should I just ask him directly about his phone behavior? I know I'm usually consoling you about this kind of stuff, but am I being too much and overreading things? I was hoping you could tell me if I'm being too sensitive or if this could be a real problem. But I just know something is off, and you know I'm not one to just look the other way!"

"You and Liam are solid as a rock, and Liam and Bryan are very different. I think you should trust that something is going on at work and he just needs to focus on his phone call. Unless there have been other things," said Deidre.

"Well, he tried to talk me out of expanding the garden and started talking about home resale value!" she retorted.

"Oh... that is kind of weird. Maybe you can ask him if something is on his mind before you jump to conclusions. I'm sure there's an explanation," said Deidre.

Alexie spent the rest of the day going over wedding plans and details in her planner. She wondered what could go wrong this close to the wedding. Liam had been supportive regarding her mother and always knew she had quirks and needed some form of therapy, but he had always been there for her. It was his idea to marry. She kept reminding herself of the real positivity within the craziness of both their lives. Liam seemed distracted by something. She hoped it wasn't a someone. She decided to trust him. She refused to let anxiety take over.

Alexie decided to run to the local nursery and create a small seasonal planter garden in another empty space. A small area where she could change out plants seasonally without a huge cost. It was another pleasant distraction. As she strolled through the aisle of tea olive bushes just to get a scent fix, her phone rang. Alexie fumbled through the bottom of her purse and missed the call. She checked the log. It was Mrs. Shelby, her childhood neighbor. She assumed she was checking on her mother. She would get back to her soon.

Chapter Nineteen- The Accidental Phone Call

Alexie returned home to Melinda and Christine. Christine's condition was rapidly declining. The old Christine rarely appeared now. It was usually the pleasant Christine wandering through the house. Alexie was fine with this new version of her mother which meant fewer triggers. She had progressed in processing her mother's secret. It helped to believe her mother had deeper issues she had never been able to face as a child or an adult, issues that caused her to lash out at those closest to her.

She decided it wasn't her job to figure out the intricacies of her mother's heart, personality, or iniquities. It happened, and she wasn't going to let it destroy, dictate, or shape the rest of her life. She thought people just do dumb stuff—just like Melinda said. Trying to analyze it without access to her mother's thinking only caused more pain. So she let it go so she could move on.

"Hey, Melinda, you have been working so hard taking care of Mom. What do you think of the adult day care center a couple miles down the road on the left? I've heard good things about it. I'm just thinking about using it for a few days when you need a break so you can spend time with your family," said Alexie.

"I think it's okay. I used it a few times for my husband, and I felt they took good care of him. Christine seemed to have a good day when we left her there that one time. How are you doing? You know... with everything?" asked Melinda.

"I'm okay. I plan on moving on. No point in dwelling on it," said Alexie.

"Oh, before I forget again... an older lady came by looking for you earlier. A Mrs. Shelby. Said she wanted to check on Christine and took a chance on stopping by. But she wanted you to get back with her—said it was very important."

"That's kind of odd for her to drive all this way. She called me today. Can you keep an eye on Mom while I call her back? I won't be but a few minutes. I'll be on the porch," said Alexie.

Alexie went outside and glanced at the new seedling tray she was preparing for a neighbor who had hired her to start a garden. She walked over to the outer porch wall and stared, arms folded, at her giant homemade dragonfly—sometimes firefly—wall artwork. She had a few brief thoughts about her grandmother and childhood, running barefoot in the dirt with an old mason jar.

Almost the best days of her life, she thought. Almost. Though this season had its challenges, she felt deeply thankful for the friends in her life and for Liam. She had learned to process her life through faith rather than despair and negativity. Here and now was the best time of her life. She smiled. Her phone rang.

"Hey, Mrs. Shelby. I was just settling down to call you. Is everything alright? I was glad you stopped by but also a bit surprised," said Alexie.

"Hey, Lexie, I'm sorry to alarm you. I wanted to see when you were available to talk. I stopped by on my way home after a bit of shopping in Columbia. It was good to see Christine for a minute. She looks well taken care of, but can we meet soon? I need to talk to you, and I need to do it before I lose my nerve. I need to tell you something. At first, I thought I should mind my own business, but it's been weighing on me. I need to tell you because I know Christine isn't able, but she wanted you to know."

"Oh, it's okay. I think I already know. Mom kept apologizing to her caretaker and talking to her as if she were me. I could never get her to tell me what she was apologizing for because of her dementia, but she told Melinda, and I found out several weeks ago," said Alexie.

"Oh, really? Wow. I was so nervous to tell you. Christine confided in me many years ago, and she said she would tell you when you were older and could understand it better. She made me promise to tell you if anything ever happened to her. She didn't think it was fair to keep it from you forever. Her mental state has been in and out for quite some time. She had a hard time handling the pressures of it all. So I wasn't going to say anything—I wanted to mind my own business—but I thought you should know because she really wanted you to know and had been waiting for the right time. But I know she can't now... anyways... I'm rambling... it would've been so hard for me to be the one to tell you your father was still alive," said Mrs. Shelby.

Alexie felt all the blood drain from her head as her breath caught short. She sank onto her bench in disbelief.

"What? WHAT did you just say? No... no... he is **not** alive! I thought you were going to tell me that my father didn't die picking me up from school. That was the secret we thought she was hiding! No... he would never—" Alexie collapsed into frantic tears as her voice rose.

"Lexie... I'm so sorry, but it's true. What do you remember about your father's funeral?" said Mrs. Shelby.

"I don't remember a funeral... I... I thought I'd blocked it out. What! How can I not know this? Does my family know? Why was this kept from me? And where has he been—does he have a family? Did he raise other kids?" cried Alexie as her voice faded.

"I'm so sorry, Lexie. Your father left home when you were a little girl and went to another state. I recently got in touch with him when Christine moved in with you. He would like to see you when you're ready—if you want to. He wants to tell you himself where he has been and why he left and hasn't been in touch. It's not what you think. Give him a chance. He had no control over it. There is a letter he wrote to you explaining everything. I left it on the mantle in your living room and asked Melinda not to give it to you until you and I had spoken."

Melinda overheard the conversation from inside the house and walked to the screen door of the back porch.

"I can't take any more of this right now. Thank you for telling me. I need time. Thank you, Mrs. Shelby," said Alexie as she hung up.

Melinda put her hand on the screen door handle and saw Alexie now sitting on the floor of the porch with her phone in her hand, in tears.

"Alexie, I overheard. You will be alright. I'm so sorry. What can I do?" said Melinda, tears welling in her eyes. She opened the door to walk toward her, but Alexie, silently overwhelmed, lifted her hand to signal that she needed to be alone.

"I'm going to take Mrs. Christine to the park to give you some time. But I am going to call Liam and Deidre to come check on you. Can I do that for you?" she asked.

Alexie nodded. She could no longer speak.

She waited until Melinda and Christine were gone and made her way to the mantle. There was a blue envelope sitting on top with Alexie's name on it—her favorite shade of blue and the same color as the tray her father had made for her as a little girl. She stared at the letter for what felt like an eternity before picking it up. She ran her fingers across the envelope. She lifted it to her nose, catching the faintest scent of smoky cologne. She fell to her knees again in tears. She still couldn't bring herself to open it.

Later in the evening she called Liam, and her call went to voicemail. He texted back saying he was in the middle of an important meeting and would come over with Emma as soon as he got off work. Another unanswered call. She set that thought aside—for now, again.

She made herself a cup of chamomile tea. She couldn't eat. She left the letter on the table and walked out to the garden carrying a storm of rage and hurt toward her mother and anyone who might have known the truth and said nothing.

She tried to plant a few seedlings, but midway through she grabbed handfuls of dirt and hurled them across the yard as tears streamed down her face. She pulled some lavender close and breathed deeply. She breathed until she was centered again.

She wandered through the garden and found herself standing beside the plant she and Emma had replanted together. Before the phone call, she had been excited to show Emma how something that had looked nearly dead now thrived. She remembered everything she'd told Emma—how the plant recovered, how it began to bear generous fruit after being uprooted and given proper sun and nutrients.

It was no longer trapped in the shade of a larger, dominant tree that had sucked away its light and strength, blocking the rain and sun it needed. Alexie and Emma had hand-pruned the brittle limbs and stripped away what was dead. The plant had survived harsh, neglectful conditions and a heavy pruning... **before it thrived.** It had even become one of the most fruitful plants of its kind in the garden once fertilized a few times.

Alexie pondered the condition of the plant now—how it flourished once it finally had what it needed.

Chapter Twenty- The Letter

My **Dearest Lexie,**

If you are reading this, then you have been told the truth—that I did not pass away, but that I am very much alive. I can't begin to explain or apologize for the pain that not knowing must have caused you. Please don't blame your mother. She was only doing what I asked, trying to protect you from what we both thought would bring you greater suffering. I am so sorry for not being in your life. Let me try to explain.

When you were a little girl, we traveled by car to Washington for a family wedding. You were riding in the back seat; your mom and I were in the front when we were blindsided and hit in the rear side by a drunk driver. We were all hurt, and I blacked out. When I came to, the driver of the other car was drunk and laughing while recording us on his phone. When I realized he hadn't called 911 for help, something in me broke.

There was a fourth person in the backseat. Your infant brother was nine months old and died in the crash. His name was Jonathan. I don't remember everything, but I was told I grabbed the driver's phone to call for help and we began to fight. I slammed his head several times onto the asphalt—far more than needed to stop him—and killed him during the scuffle. The jury saw it as a vengeful act for harming my family.

I was in prison for decades and was only recently released. Your mother agreed to tell you I had passed because I didn't want you to see me in jail. Most of your adult relatives knew but promised not to tell their children, to help keep the secret. Over time, your mother and I lost contact; she stopped visiting a few years into my sentence. It was too painful for her, and she was grieving Jonathan. After four years in prison, I received divorce papers from your mother. I begged her to move on. I didn't want her or you to carry the burden of my imprisonment. She didn't understand at first and felt I was choosing to leave her to protect you, but I had you both in mind.

I recently saw your mother, and it was too much for her—a painful reminder of the night we lost Jonathan. It was so upsetting that I pulled back, but I still felt compelled to ease my way back into her life somehow. I could see what the years had done to her. I want you to know I would like to see you in time, but only when and if you are ready. I have no intention of disrupting your life.

I am deeply sorry that I didn't have the self-control to think through my actions the night I took someone's life. I considered not contacting you at all, but I hoped we could have the next thirty years to rebuild what we once had. I am sorry that my choices changed the trajectory of your life and childhood. I hope you can find it in your heart to forgive me—and those who vowed to keep our secret.

I will go at whatever pace you need as we rebuild our connection. Please call when you are ready to talk or visit.

Love,
Your Dad,
Steven

Alexie sat stunned into numbness. She shoved the photo back into the envelope, unable to bear looking at it. Could the dreams that had plagued her for years be fractured memories of that night? The crying she remembered—were they not her cries, but the cries of her infant brother?

She sat on the living room floor for hours, trying to piece together faint memories of the brother who had simply vanished from her childhood. There had been no trace of a nursery. No pictures. Christine had erased every reminder of her grief, converting the nursery into another room and removing all photographs of her son. It had been too much for her to bear, and the weight of it began her slow mental decline. Alexie, so young at the time, had blocked out almost everything.

She read the letter again in disbelief. Then she slowly crumpled it into a ball and threw it into the corner of the room.

Alexie grabbed her keys and drove to the park, circling it more times than she could count. She eventually found the prettiest view near the amphitheater and sat silently as darkness settled over the day.

Melinda grew concerned and contacted Liam, telling him what had happened as they tried to figure out where she had gone, since Alexie ignored their calls. Melinda and Deidre felt sure she was at the lake, but Liam was certain she would be at the park—and he was right.

He found her sitting alone in the dark. She had nothing left to say, and no tears left to give. Liam wrapped his jacket around her and sat quietly beside her until the sun rose. Then he walked her to his car and drove her home as she finally drifted into sleep.

Weeks passed, and Alexie spent more time than ever in the garden, the park, and at the lake. She took on every project she could to distract herself from fully processing the truth. She launched a new income stream in her business: planning and starting raised-bed gardens for people. The money was great, and the plant therapy was even better. She felt she couldn't take another of life's surprises and prayed there were no more coming. Her view of her mother had shifted—still not excusing her abuse, but understanding its roots. She still hadn't contacted her father... yet. She needed time. She needed space. She needed support.

Liam had been her anchor through it all. He listened, comforted, and gave her space—even when she needed time to avoid processing entirely. As their wedding drew closer, she was convinced he was the right man for her. Still, she fought back suspicions stirred by his recent behaviors. She couldn't handle another relational blow, and she knew he understood that. She trusted that his actions were for her good.

Trust was the only thing she had energy left for.

Chapter Twenty-One-
Fertilizer

Liam had dropped off Emma for some long-awaited and needed girl time between the two of them. Emma had grown distant from her mother while staying with Liam—the healthy amount of distance needed to begin processing and healing. Emma lay on the back porch bench with her knees up, talking on the phone. As Alexie entered the porch, Emma ended her conversation.

They walked out to the garden, picked specific herbs, placed them in the pre-warmed oven, then pulled out several skinny spice jars from the cabinet before returning to the porch.

"I was talking to Dad, and I think I want to be a horticulturist one day—like you! How long did you go to school for it?" Emma asked while pulling her hair into a messy bun.

"I have a degree in an unrelated field. I took classes for a few months to learn about plants and planting, including hands-on training from Tess at the nursery. I'm thinking about getting another degree related to plant science. We'll see. But you can go to college for horticulture or agriculture, or even get an advanced degree in botany if you want. Maybe start thinking about how you'd use your knowledge to educate and help people. Think about what part you love most. You still have time to decide on a major," said Lexie.

They had harvested a small number of herbs—rosemary, cilantro, Thai lemon basil, and a few others—and placed them in the oven on low heat to dry quickly. They crushed them using her grandmother's old mortar and pestle, pouring the spices into empty glass bottles as they talked. Alexie often gave bottles of homemade dried spices as gifts.

"Yeah. I'm so sure this is what I want to study. I guess I do have time to hone it in. Have you ever thought about selling your ground spices? Or maybe teaching classes on how to dry and mix them? That mix was really good on the chicken and veggies Dad made last week!"

"I actually have thought about selling them, but I hadn't considered teaching classes on how to make dried spices. That would be a fun offshoot of the business. And since it was your idea, I just might name it after you—Emma's Tablespice Classes or maybe Emma's Corner. We can design the spice bottle label together. What do you think? You can assist me in the classes!" said Alexie while crushing dried rosemary.

"Oh wow! You would name it after me? Let me know when we start!" Emma gushed, her ears turning red with emotion.

"Yeah, let's sit down and plan it out next week. The wedding planning is almost done, so I'll have more free time. Emma, you look good. You look happy and adjusted to being in a new town. But how are you feeling... like on the inside... in your head... and about seeing your mom in court when your dad—I mean—when we get full custody of you?" asked Alexie while funneling spices into jars.

"In my head? Um... I'm not sure. No one has ever really asked me how I was doing in that way before. I'm thankful to be here with y'all. I don't feel stressed unless Mom calls. I want to live with y'all. I have trouble figuring out what I feel, but I can tell you what I think pretty well," Emma said, pressing harder into the spice grinding.

After finishing, they walked back out to the garden to the plant they had planted, pruned, and fertilized.

"I still can't believe it did so well. It looks the best out of all of them. That's amazing!" said Emma.

"Yep, it's doing quite well. After we pruned and replanted it, I added a little fertilizer and massaged it into the dirt. It was doing well before, but the fertilizer made it take off. It went through a lot—kind of like us. We went through a lot... before we thrived. And now look at us," said Alexie.

"Us? You've mentioned before that we *both* went through a lot," said Emma with curiosity.

"So, it's almost time for the appointment. Let's go. I have some things I want to share with you about my childhood and some other things I recently learned," said Alexie, grabbing her keys from the wall hook.

On the way to the appointment, Alexie shared her childhood circumstances, details about her relationship with her mother, and as much of the newly revealed family secret as she felt Emma could understand.

"Wow... I hate that you went through all that... and here I thought my family was the only one all jacked up! Oh—sorry! I didn't mean *you* were jacked up... just your situation..." Emma covered her face in embarrassment.

Alexie laughed. "No worries! I know exactly what you meant. I'm not offended. So—we're here. Remember, just relax and talk about whatever's on your mind. You'll learn to process your feelings in time. Trust me, I know."

They pulled into the parking lot of New Horizon Christian Therapies and Intervention. They got out of the car and walked into the waiting room.

Emma looked back at Alexie, confused. "Are you going in with me to talk to my therapist?"

"No. I'm going into the other room to see a different therapist for myself. I need a little fertilizer too—like our plant, right?" said Alexie.

"Right! I get it. See you in an hour," Emma said with reassurance in her voice.

Chapter Twenty-Two-
Liam's Distraction and
Inheritance

They arrived back home after their very first therapy sessions. Liam was waiting enthusiastically on the porch, but he didn't dare ask how it went. He would wait until—or if—they were ready to discuss it. He noticed that Emma seemed a bit lighter in spirit. Alexie winked at him as they walked past on the front porch. Emma headed for her favorite spot out back, settled into her hammock, and called her friend.

Liam asked Alexie to sit with him on the front porch to talk about something. Her heart began to race. She wondered what he could possibly want to discuss. *Here it comes,* she thought. *Maybe he wants to put off the wedding. Maybe it's all becoming too much for him.*

"Hey, it was good to see you both come back smiling. I have something I want to run by you," Liam said, pulling a rolled-up poster tube from underneath the chair.

"I know you love this house—or rather, you love this yard, with all the work and details you've put into the plantings and garden. Remember my aunt, the one who didn't have children and passed away not long ago? Well, I've been on the phone settling her estate, and she left me almost everything as her oldest nephew. My family owns several miles of acreage where it's nothing but our relatives for miles down the road. My aunt left me many acres. It's only thirty minutes from here, so you could still see your friends as usual, but we'd shop in Blythewood—where Kevin doesn't live or shop. He wouldn't be able to ride by your door and wave or intimidate you, because there's a beautiful house sitting on nine acres of wooded, green, hilly land. It's perfect for gardening.

"We could move into that house, or we could build our own with a long driveway so nobody can just drive by. We wouldn't have to worry about Kevin trying to buy the house down the street to harass us because my relatives own the surrounding acres and would never sell. It's still suburban living with a serving of country on the side—farming if you want it—close to the city and shopping. I've been working with Tess to draw up this map and duplicate your present backyard."

Liam unrolled the landscape plan—an exact replica of Alexie's backyard, down to every plant, tree, bush, and swing—and showed it to her.

"I know you're not really attached to the house... it's the yard you love. We now have enough money to pull up and replant anything you want and place it exactly how you want it in a new backyard. And we can replace anything that won't survive being moved. I also put a restraining order on Kevin. We can get married on our new property and not worry about him crashing the wedding and making a scene. There are a couple of smaller houses on the property where we can house your mom, and we can afford around-the-clock in-home care. It would mean seeing less of Kevin and having the backyard you've worked for so long to build—and then some. Whatever your decision, I will—"

Alexie put her hands over her face. Liam stopped talking.

She finally said, "Yes. Let's do it!" and hugged him.

That warm, secure feeling washed over her again—the strongest wave yet. The feeling of being loved and cared for beyond anything she had ever expected. A feeling she still couldn't fully put into words.

"I'm sorry. I should've waited to spring this on you, but I knew you could tell I was acting weird, and I didn't want to cause you any more anxiety. You've been through enough. I've been busy on the phone with estate lawyers and Tess," he said, unsure of what she was thinking.

"Is this what you've been whispering about for weeks? You've been talking to Tess to duplicate the yard?! I can't believe you'd recreate the entire backyard. It's like sixty-seven bushes and trees and all the garden beds! I think since we have all that acreage, I'll keep my present plan and add to it. But I *am* taking my tea olive bushes—and a few more trees," she said, sliding the plans from his hands.

They made their way to the backyard to go over the landscape design and then told Emma about the new plan. The new property was big enough for everyone to have their own appropriate space—even Melinda, who could live on-site as a caretaker for Christine. To say they were excited was an understatement. They all leaped into the car to go visit the new property.

And their story didn't end here... Could there be greener grass in Blythewood? Was Alexie about to marry a millionaire farmer?

Book Two of the Ballentine Lake Murray Resilience Series

BOOK TWO OF THE BALLENTINE Lake Murray Resilience Series will explore Alexie's and Liam's wedding and new property, problems and progress. It will explore Emma and Lisa, Carla, Bryan and Deidre and new characters. It will explore Christine and Alexie's father. Maybe Kevin. Maybe not. It will reveal a new way of life with ups and downs, laughter and tears, and little drama as they continue to live their lives married on a new farmland property. It will explore and visit areas of Greenville, areas withing Columbia, Charleston, Irmo, Blythewood, Prosperity, Newberry and more. Escape with me into their relationships, lives, and experiences in Book Two of the Ballentine Lake Murray Southern Resilience Series.

Please visit www.DeannaTCove.com[1] for reader contest details with a chance to write a few lines of descriptive scenery, describe or select the appearance of a new character, or name a new family pet in Book Two out soon! Please sign up on my site for more books and blog updates coming soon. Thank you and please leave a positive review on your purchase platform!

Please visit my website to sign up for my free no obligation newsletter, check out my blog and stay updated for any new releases!

WWW.DEANNATCOVE.COM[2]

---

1.   http://www.DeannaTCove.com

2. http://www.DeannaTCove.com

About the Author

Deanna T. Cove resides in the Midlands of South Carolina with her husband of thirty-seven years. Together they have three adult children and two grandchildren. Deanna retired from the field of nursing years ago and developed a new love of gardening. Her passion for writing began in childhood as she attended and tested into Mark Twain JHS for the Gifted and Talented in New York with creative writing as her talent.

Though born in the north Deanna considers herself to be a southern lady with family ties to the south through generations. Deanna moved south at the age of fifteen and developed a deep love for the south and weaves her travels of neighboring cities into her storylines. After retiring from the medical field, she was a top selling copywriter and business branding expert freelancing with Fiverr.com for nearly two years working with businesses worldwide before retiring to other styles of writing.

...Before We Thrived... is her first of many novels, series and more.

Read more at www.DeannaTCove.com.